Ou...
Three ....m!

When Princ....... ...ll in love and stepped out of the line of succession, the lives of his three sisters changed irrevocably.

Princess Gisella became the crown princess, and her younger sisters, Beatrix and Cecelia, were expected to step even further into the royal spotlight and carry the monarchy into the future.

But as they await their brother's royal wedding and Gisella's coronation, the princesses all begin to question their place in the palace and discover that their true hearts' desires might not be exactly as they imagined...

Read Cecelia and Antoine's story in
His Accidentally Pregnant Princess
Available now!

Watch out for Beatrix's and Gisella's stories, coming soon!

Dear Reader,

I'm so excited to share with you the Princesses of Rydiania series. The princesses were initially introduced in *It Started with a Royal Kiss*. They so intrigued me that I had to tell their stories, especially now that big changes are afoot in the palace.

To start things off, Her Royal Highness Princess Cecelia has just been dumped by her boyfriend. Yes, even princesses experience heartbreak. Now the princess needs a moment away from the spotlight to indulge in some ice cream and binge-watch television.

Businessman Antoine Dupre has inherited his grandparents' vineyard in the South of France. The château is full of dust and unhappy memories, and Antoine is determined to fix up the large home and sell it. After all, he never intends to have a family of his own.

When their paths cross in Saint-Tropez, things get turned upside down. An accident leaves Cecelia with amnesia and Antoine is there to help her, offering her a job as his housekeeper. As Cecelia dusts and mops, she uncovers clues to Antoine's own past. But when Cecelia remembers her real name, will it ruin any chance they have at happiness?

Happy reading!

Jennifer

His Accidentally Pregnant Princess

Jennifer Faye

Recycling programs
for this product may
not exist in your area.

ISBN-13: 978-1-335-73709-0

His Accidentally Pregnant Princess

Copyright © 2023 by Jennifer F. Stroka

For questions and comments about the quality of this book,
please contact us at CustomerService@Harlequin.com.

Harlequin Enterprises ULC
22 Adelaide St. West, 41st Floor
Toronto, Ontario M5H 4E3, Canada
www.Harlequin.com

Printed in U.S.A.

Award-winning author **Jennifer Faye** pens fun contemporary romances. Internationally published with books translated into more than a dozen languages, she is a two-time winner of the *RT Book Reviews* Reviewers' Choice Award and winner of the CataRomance Reviewers' Choice Award. Now living her dream, she resides with her very patient husband and Writer Kitty. When she's not plotting out her next romance, you can find her with a mug of tea and a book. Learn more at jenniferfaye.com.

Books by Jennifer Faye

Harlequin Romance

Greek Paradise Escape

Greek Heir to Claim Her Heart
It Started with a Royal Kiss
Second Chance with the Bridesmaid

Wedding Bells at Lake Como

Bound by a Ring and a Secret
Falling for Her Convenient Groom

The Bartolini Legacy

The CEO, the Puppy and Me
The Italian's Unexpected Heir

Fairytale Christmas with the Millionaire

Visit the Author Profile page
at Harlequin.com for more titles.

CHAPTER ONE

Her plan was in motion…

With a totally new hair color and style, as well as the addition of big dark sunglasses, a blue ball cap and a casual wardrobe, Princess Cecelia of Rydiania had been transformed from a trendsetter to just another person in the crowd.

It was a tall order for sure. And that's why she'd gone above and beyond any of her other prior disguises to the point of cutting off the signature, long golden-brown locks that she'd had all of her life. Her hair was now styled in a short, sleek, bleached-blond pageboy style. She had been very nervous about the stark change in her appearance, but it was slowly growing on her. The queen, on the other hand, would have a coronary the next time she saw her youngest daughter, but Cecelia would deal with that later.

On this early June morning, Cecelia waited

in a small private airport. She lowered her sunglasses to look around. Not a soul was glancing in her direction. She breathed a bit easier.

She reached for her compact one more time. She snapped it open to inspect her appearance. Her friend had applied her heavy, dark eye makeup. Cecelia had never worn this much in her life. She was more inclined to wear a light layer in earth tones.

Her bulky costume jewelry had her looking like she was ready for a night of partying, which was quite the opposite of her plans. She'd paired it with faded jeans and a black strappy top she'd sewn herself on a sewing machine in her suite of rooms. Black wasn't her favorite go-to color, but in this instance, she didn't want to stand out. She wanted an outfit that would make her fade into the background.

She returned the compact to her purse and then withdrew her phone. She wasn't so reckless as to disappear without leaving word with her family. The last thing her family needed was another scandal. Her brother had certainly turned the royal household on its head when he'd walked away from being heir to the throne.

In truth, she initially hadn't believed the news. Istvan was a rule follower—a people pleaser. Or at least she'd thought so. It seemed there was more to her brother than she'd known. She applauded his ability to stand up for himself, but it was the fallout that had her and her sisters making daily royal appearances. And after her recent romantic breakup, she needed some time to herself.

She tried to think of whom to message at the palace. Absolutely not her security team. They'd probably track her phone and catch up with her before her flight took off.

As for the king, he might understand. She was the youngest and he let her get away with more things than her other siblings. But her father didn't carry his own phone.

And certainly not the queen, as they weren't that close. While her father would indulge Cecelia, her mother was strict and expected protocols to be followed at all times. Her eldest sister, Gisella, was a lot like their mother. Duty first and everything else, including family, a distant second.

And that left her middle sister, Beatrix. She was closest to her middle sister. Beatrix was a born peacemaker. And over the years, the four royal heirs had needed someone to help keep the peace. Hopefully her sister would help her out.

Hey. Can you do me a favor?

Almost immediately there was a reply from Beatrix.

What do you need?

Tonight at dinner can you tell Mother and Father that I went on holiday?

What?

I just need a couple of weeks to get my head on straight.

You mean because of the breakup?

Yes.

I understand. What about security?

I can take care of myself.

Sure you can. *eye-roll emoji*

I can!

Where does your security think you are?

At a friend's.

You can't keep doing this. Mother is going to flip out.

Don't worry. In two weeks I'll be back doing royal appearances.

She could already envision the frown on her sister's face. Beatrix didn't like to break the rules. Cecelia felt bad for putting her in this situation. When the time came, she'd pay her sister back.

Is there anything that will change your mind?

No. I need this. See you soon.

Be careful.

Always.

After that, she pulled the battery from her phone and stuffed it in her purse. Just that small act had her feeling so much freer. Now it was time to board a friend's private jet for France.

Everything was going according to plan...

She took her seat and settled in. She chose

the seat next to the window. The plane's owner wasn't a particularly close friend. And she had a new guy in her life that kept her occupied with a lot of PDA. Cecelia turned away, taking the time to unwind.

While she loved being with her family, she didn't love having thousands of people staring at her on a daily basis while the tabloids chronicled her life. And when there wasn't anything interesting going on, they fabricated stories.

As much as people wanted to believe that you got used to such things, you didn't. It was uncomfortable having her every word, choice and activity scrutinized. Now her romantic life, or lack thereof, was being splashed across the internet with the most cringeworthy headlines.

As a young child, she'd been scared to have a bunch of people rushing toward her, calling out her name. While she'd overcome that fear, she still wasn't at ease in front of a crowd. Still, she did what royal duty dictated.

She remembered as a child being out in public. The queen had gently reprimanded Cecelia for not sitting still. In turn, Cecelia may have stuck out her tongue at her mother in rebellion. She vividly recalled thumbing her nose at her mother and wiggling her fingers. They had been at the royal orchestra. And for a child, it was the most boring torture. And to be honest, she still found those events boring. Luckily, after that event was publicized in all of the Rydianian papers, Cecelia's attendance had been rarely requested until she got older.

However, things had recently changed when Istvan had fallen in love with a commoner and stepped out of the line of succession in order to marry. Talk about creating drama, and not only in the palace, but also throughout the kingdom that was nestled between France, Switzerland and Italy. Though the dominant language of the kingdom was French, Cecelia and her siblings were multilingual.

Cecelia thought her homeland was one of the most beautiful countries in all of Europe. The land was lush and laws had been passed to protect much of the land's natural beauty. The Rydianian people were the best with their kind and thoughtful ways. If it wasn't for the incessant press, she wouldn't have any desire to leave Rydiania.

She wasn't the only one in the family to be hounded by the paparazzi. The tabloids were constantly comparing Istvan to their late uncle, who had abdicated the throne years ago. After their uncle was banished from Rydiania, he ended up moving to the small Greek island of Ludus, where he'd spent the remainder of his years.

Thankfully Istvan had stepped out of the line of succession before he was crowned. Therefore it was not necessary to banish him from the kingdom. Cecelia was most grateful. She couldn't imagine life without her big brother in it.

But with her brother stepping aside, everything within the palace had changed. Their father, the king, now had to stay on the throne even though his physical ailments grew worse by the day. Her sister Gisella needed time to get up to speed with everything her life would entail as queen. It was quite an undertaking to move from the spare heir to the crown princess.

The palace's PR staff worked round-the-clock to put out the headlines of a finely run monarchy, even if it was anything but calm. In the past eight months, since Istvan had made up his mind to quit the family business, she had been called upon to step up as a working royal.

It was a position she'd only ever taken up on occasion when her older siblings were unavailable, which wasn't often. Now she was called on most every day to make appearances at various foundation luncheons, gallery openings and film debuts.

And though from the outside it may sound like a glamorous life, and she knew she was very fortunate for the life she'd been born into, it didn't make it easier to be constantly in front of the cameras. The press insisted on analyzing her every action, from how she wore her hair to photographing the people she interacted with—they were always on the lookout for someone to link her with romantically.

Trying to have a meaningful relationship while in the spotlight was virtually impossible. And yet, she'd fooled herself into believing she could have it all—the tiara, the status as a royal and true love. And now she had a broken heart to prove her wrong.

Paul Van Horne was a friend of a friend. With great hesitation on both sides, they'd been set up on a blind date. And to their great surprise, they'd hit it off, despite the fact that Paul was a private person and her life was anything but private.

However, they learned that they read some of the same thrillers and even a few cozy mysteries. Instead of mourning the fashion degree she'd been forced to give up in order to live a life of service, she found reading something she could do in the car, or while waiting to make a scheduled appearance. It didn't replace her love of sewing, but it was a welcome distraction.

She would phone Paul in the evening when she'd discovered a new author. He, in turn, would do the same for her. It was the bond on which their relationship began to blossom.

Paul liked action movies and she found that she did, too. They would wait and enter the theater after the lights were dimmed and slip back out just before the lights came back on. In most cases, it meant missing the very end of a movie, but they weren't ready to share their newfound relationship with the rest of the world.

For a couple of months, they'd kept their relationship on the down low, except for a select few friends that were sworn to secrecy.

And then, a week ago, she hadn't been quite so careful and the paparazzi had followed her. Unbeknownst to her and Paul, they'd been photographed holding hands as they entered the theater. The Duchess Tales, the county's biggest royal gossip site, posted a photo of them kissing inside Paul's car.

The next morning, her phone awoke her before dawn. Once she'd realized it was Paul, her irritation subsided. A smile tugged at her lips as she'd answered the phone. She was certain he'd had as good a time as her.

But when she'd pressed the phone to her ear, Paul rambled on so quickly that it was hard to tell what he was saying. In the end, she figured out that the paparazzi had followed him home and were camped out in front of his apartment. She'd apologized and calmed him down.

As the days went by, the reporters became more aggressive. They contacted Paul's employer, his parents and siblings. They even knocked on his neighbors' doors and contacted his ex-girlfriends.

Paul called her again. It was over.

He refused to put himself and those close to him through the constant interrogation. She'd wanted to ask him to give them more time, but she knew time wouldn't change anything.

He said he was sorry, but it did nothing to ease the ache in her chest. She didn't think she'd ever find someone to love her through the good and the bad.

And so, with a broken heart in need of mending, Cecelia had made a decision. She was going away. She craved a location where no one knew her—someplace where the reporters wouldn't find her and inquire about

Paul's absence. Because as of now, she was done with men.

When she'd tried to explain to the queen that she didn't want to go out in public for a while, her mother waved off her concerns like it was no big deal. Cecelia didn't say it at the time, but it hurt to have her emotions so readily dismissed.

Instead, her mother had reminded her that the royal wedding was coming up and everyone must give a hundred and ten percent until then. The queen painstakingly planned every detail, so it would be an event no one would forget. They would show the world a united family that Cecelia wasn't so sure existed, or maybe she was just growing frustrated with all of the pomp and circumstance. And so, piece by piece, she concocted her plan to step out of the spotlight until her disastrous dating life slipped from the headlines.

A couple of hours passed before Cecelia was at last in Saint-Tropez. The sun was shining but even it couldn't get her to smile. She planned to be in France for two weeks. She wasn't even sure she wanted to leave her hotel suite during her stay. She might just order room service and drown her sorrows in chocolate-chip ice cream and junk food while binge-watching television in order to forget her own real-life drama.

First, she had to check in. She'd made reservations at a new hotel under a false name. Somehow the reservation had gotten messed up and they didn't have a room available for her. Now she had to try another hotel.

Her driver recommended another boutique hotel. But as the car made its way to the front entrance of the hotel, she immediately noticed the throng of paparazzi. Her chest tightened. Were they there for her? Impossible. She wasn't even supposed to be staying at this hotel.

"Don't stop here," she told the driver. "Keep going a little way."

She wasn't about to test her disguise with the paparazzi—at least not willingly and certainly not on her very first day. Farther down the road, she asked the driver to pull over.

Now standing on the sidewalk with her luggage in hand, she had to find a way to check in to the hotel. She decided to try the back entrance. It was how she came and went from other hotels during high-profile events.

And so she started walking. Brand-new heeled sandals probably weren't the best choice for today. Her feet started to ache. She would change into something more comfortable once she checked into her room.

When she reached the alley behind the hotel, she was relieved to find it empty. She continued down the narrow alleyway with her suitcase rumbling along behind her. When she came to the steps that led up to the back door, she tried to pull her suitcase up the steps without success. Instead, she had to pick it up. Normally that wouldn't have been such a big deal, but this time she'd overpacked and it weighed a ton.

She struggled up the steps, all the while telling herself to pack less the next time she went on holiday. Just then a young man came rushing out of the hotel. He moved swiftly, like the devil himself was hot on his trail.

On his way down the steps, he reached out and grabbed Cecelia's purse strap.

And this was where her well-laid plan began to unravel...

Instinctively, she tightened her fingers around the purse strap. She wasn't prepared for the man to jerk so hard. Her body swayed to the side.

Everything started to move in slow motion as she lost her balance. The heavy suitcase rolled back. With her fingers still around the handle, the weight of the case pulled her down the steps. Her feet went out from under her. The air rushed from her lungs as she let out a cry.

CHAPTER TWO

HIS MEETING HAD CONCLUDED.

Antoine Dupré was pleased with himself. The hotel was willing to buy some of this autumn's wine. It wouldn't be a large harvest, but it would be enough to sell locally. It would show potential buyers the value in the land.

Since inheriting his family's vineyard, he'd taken time away from his ever-growing business in Paris to return to his childhood home, and had spent the last couple of months revitalizing the fields closest to the château while taming the more distant fields that had sustained some neglect. He strived to restore the vineyard's award-winning name.

After leaving home to head off to university, he'd never planned to return to the vineyard to live. He'd had a huge row with his grandfather and he hadn't seen his grandmother after that. At her funeral, he'd promised himself that he'd never toil in dirt again.

It's funny how saying "never" was like tempting fate to prove you wrong.

He'd been raised at the Dupré Vineyard. When his mother died in childbirth, his grandparents had taken him home with them, since his father's identity was unknown.

His grandfather had been a hard man. He had unyielding rules and if you broke them, you were punished. It was no wonder his mother had been trying to find a way out of the vineyard. Too bad she'd turned to a man who'd impregnated her and then disappeared, leaving her to deal with the fallout. Because even though pregnancy outside of marriage was more common back in those days, it was still frowned upon by his grandparents.

Antoine had grown up with a desire not to be reliant on anyone. He was certain that once he gained his financial freedom, he would be happy. And though he'd built his empire from the ground up, Dupré Enterprises and his vast fortune still didn't fulfill him. There was something missing from his life, but he couldn't put his finger on it.

As he headed toward the hotel's front entrance, he saw a crowd of people through the large windows. As he looked closer, he noticed a great number of them were holding cameras. *Paparazzi.*

He had no idea why they were outside the hotel and he had no intention of finding out. He pivoted in the opposite direction.

Ding.

He reached for his phone as he headed out the back exit. He used his phone exclusively to manage his business. He wasn't one to scroll through social media—he didn't even have a social-media account. Unless it was business news or stock prices, he didn't have time for it.

He looked at the phone's screen to find a message from one of his vice presidents. He opened the email and began to read. Antoine was engrossed in the message as he started down the outside steps. And then something out of the corner of his eye caught his attention.

He lowered his phone to find a young woman lying at the bottom of the steps. She was facedown. Her arms were spread wide, as though she'd tried to catch herself and failed.

He rushed toward her.

He kneeled down beside her. Her sunglasses had fallen off. And there was an angry gash on the side of her temple. Blood trickled down her face.

The whole left side of her face was scraped. The skin was red and already starting to swell. Both of her eyes were closed. That wasn't good. His breath hitched in his throat as he checked for a pulse. When he found one, he let out a breath.

"Miss? Miss? Can you hear me?" He started dialing for help.

She didn't move. His instinct was to pick her up and move her inside the hotel, where it would be more comfortable, but he hesitated. He knew enough about injuries not to move someone who might have sustained a spinal injury. He certainly didn't want to make matters worse.

He talked to the operator and the agonizing wait began. With each passing moment she was unconscious, his worry mounted. How long did it take for an ambulance to arrive? It seemed to be taking forever. A couple of hotel employees must have heard the noise and came rushing over to lend their assistance. He sent them to wait at the main road for the ambulance and then to guide it into the alleyway.

Second by second, minute by minute, she was lying there on the concrete as though she was sleeping—like some fairy-tale princess. The thing about fairy tales was that they didn't have happy endings—not unless they were Americanized versions. He wanted this young woman to have a happy ending.

By then more people had taken notice of the situation. He didn't have time to worry about who saw what or took photos. Right now, his full concentration was on the young woman with the blood oozing from the cut on her temple.

"Here." Someone behind him leaned over and offered him a white cloth.

He grabbed it and pressed it to the wound. Time seemed to crawl along as they waited for the ambulance. His sleeping beauty still hadn't shown any signs of waking up. This wasn't good. Not good at all.

"Come on. Open your eyes," he coaxed.

When at last the wail of the siren could be heard in the distance, he breathed a little easier. She just had to be alright.

He didn't know this woman's name or anything about her. He was quite certain he'd never laid eyes on her before, but suddenly everything else in his world had fallen to the background. He had to be certain she was alright.

Her head hurt. *A lot*.

She opened her eyes. The bright white light had her closing them again. What was going on? Where was she?

Her mind felt foggy. She tried to remember where she was but came up with no answer.

When she attempted to open her eyes again, she lifted only one eyelid ever so slightly. And then she opened the other eye. She blinked as she looked around. Was she in a doctor's office? No. It was a hospital room.

A hospital room?

Panic engulfed her. She struggled to sit up. Her head felt heavy and it hurt so much. She moved too quickly and the room swayed to the side. Her stomach took a nauseous dip.

"Hey. It's alright." A deep male voice spoke gently to her as a hand came to rest on her lower arm.

She turned her head and was met by the most intense brown eyes. They were the shade of an early summer morning—the kind of day where there was a gentle breeze with just a puffy white cloud floating through the wide-open sky. They stared back at her with concern reflected in them.

Her gaze took in his short, light brown hair, which was swept off to one side. His strong jaw had a bit of scruff over it, and he had the beginnings of a mustache. It suited him and gave him an air of strength.

His broad shoulders looked muscular, as though they were capable of carrying the weight of the world. Her immediate instinct was that she could trust him. But as she tried to put a name to the handsome face, she found herself unable to do so.

Her heart beat faster. Who was this man? He wasn't wearing a white coat, so he probably wasn't a doctor. So why was he in her hospital room? She was so confused. Why couldn't she remember anything?

She yanked her arm away from his touch. She slid over to the far side of her bed. In fluent French, she asked, "Who are you?"

He leaned back as though realizing he'd startled her. "I'm sorry. I didn't mean to scare you. My name is Antoine Dupré."

The name meant absolutely nothing to her. She attempted to search her memory, but her head hurt and she was having problems thinking. "Do we know each other?"

He shook his head. "No. We don't."

"Then what are you doing here?"

"I was there when you fell and I wanted to make sure you're alright." His gaze was filled with genuine concern. "Do you have family or a friend that I can call for you?"

"I, uh…" She tried to recall her parents but her thoughts were foggy. She couldn't see their faces or remember their names. "I don't know."

"Don't know?" His eyebrows drew together. "What don't you know?"

Frustration bunched up in her gut. "Everything."

How could she not know her own parents' names? Who forgot something like that? If only her head would stop pounding, she was certain she could recall their names.

"Maybe we should start at the beginning." His voice drew her from her thoughts. "What is your name?"

That was a simple enough question. She opened her mouth to answer him but nothing came out. She drew another blank. She pressed her lips together in a firm line. This couldn't be happening.

"I—I don't know." She kept trying to draw the information from her jumbled thoughts.

"Just give it a moment. You had quite the fall. It'll come to you." His voice was deep as he tried to soothe her.

As she grew increasingly frustrated, she scrunched her eyes closed. She tried to get past the foggy barrier in her mind. It was proving fruitless. Panic clawed at the back of her throat. What was happening to her?

"Hey. Calm down." He went to reach out to her but then pulled his hand back. "It's going to be okay."

Did he really believe that? Because right at that moment, nothing was okay. She couldn't recall anything about herself or her past, so everything was very far from okay.

Just then, a short, older man with a few strands of snow-white hair stepped into the room. "Ah, good. You're awake. You gave us quite a start. How are you feeling?"

"I don't know my name." The rest of the scrapes, aches and bruises didn't matter in that moment. She had to know who she was. "Do you know my name?"

The doctor shook his head. "I'm afraid we don't. We were hoping when you woke up that you would be able to tell us that."

And then, a thought came to her. "I must have had a purse with me or a phone. It will have my identity."

The doctor consulted the digital notebook in his hand. "You didn't come in with either of those items."

The man beside her, what was his name? Antoine. He cleared his throat. "I'm afraid you didn't have your purse when I found you."

She tried to recall what had occurred, but it was a blank. How could she forget something that traumatic? It had just happened, hadn't it?

"How long have I been here?" she asked.

"An hour or so," Antoine said.

She turned to the doctor. "What's wrong with me?"

"Well, you took a pretty serious blow to the head when you fell, which would explain your amnesia."

"When will I get my memory back?"

"It's hard to say. Each case is different. We also had to put in some stitches. You also have a broken nose. It's causing a lot of facial swelling and bruising. But don't worry, it should all heal in time."

She reached for her forehead and felt the bandage. She lowered her hand to her nose, where there was more dressing. "Will it leave a scar?"

She didn't know why she had asked that. In the grand scheme of things, it didn't seem like such an important point. And yet there was something deep within her that said it was a very big deal.

Then a worrisome thought came to her. Was she one of those vain people who worried about their appearance above all else? Yet if that was the case, why hadn't she freaked out about the ugly hospital gown they'd put her in?

She let out a sigh. Nothing was making sense.

"You are in luck," the doctor said. "We had

one of our finest plastic surgeons available. He was able to do the stitches and set your nose. He says that in time you'll barely be able to see the scar."

Why did his answer give her great comfort? She was vain. She inwardly groaned. It wasn't good when you learned things about yourself that you didn't like. What else wouldn't she like about herself?

"When can I leave?" She didn't like hospitals. She didn't know if she had bad memories of one, or if it was just being in a hospital that she didn't like. Either way, she was more than ready to leave.

"You took quite a blow, and I would like to keep you under observation for twenty-four hours to be sure there's nothing more serious going on." He gazed at her over the top of his black-rimmed reading glasses. "Do you hurt anywhere else?"

"I feel like I got run over, but I don't think it's anything serious. Just a bunch of aches."

The doctor nodded. "We took a number of X-rays but didn't see anything worrisome. But if something changes and you feel worse, let the nurse know."

She nodded. "I will."

And then the doctor was gone. She was once again alone with the impossibly handsome Frenchman. Why was he lingering? He didn't know her. She didn't even know herself.

Her gaze met his. And for a second there was a jolt in her chest as though her heart had skipped a beat and then resumed.

She wet her dry lips and noticed how his eyes widened. It took her a moment to find her voice. "Thank you for helping me out. I really do appreciate it. But you don't have to stay any longer."

His eyebrows rose at her dismissal. He seemed as if he was about to turn and leave but then he turned back to her. "What will you do now?"

"I guess I'll be staying here overnight."

"I meant after that. You have no money. And no way of contacting your family."

He was right. She had absolutely no idea, but she wasn't going to let him see her desperation. "I'll figure out something."

"Is there anything I can do?"

She shook her head and immediately regretted it. Her head was pounding. Right now, she just wanted some pain relievers and to close her eyes. Maybe when she woke up, the world would have righted itself. She could only hope.

"No. Thank you."

He nodded, even though a look of reservation appeared on his tanned face. "I'll leave my number at the nurses' station just in case you need anything." He hesitated a moment longer before he said, "Goodbye."

And then he was gone. All alone in the room, she felt the intensity of her situation. She felt so alone…and scared. Maybe she shouldn't have been so quick to dismiss Antoine's help. After all, what was she going to do with no memory and no money?

CHAPTER THREE

HE COULDN'T STOP thinking of her.

The next morning, Antoine had gone out early to work on the vines. He'd had a restless night. His dreams had been filled with the mysterious blonde from yesterday. One dream turned into a nightmare where she fell right in front of him and he tried to catch her, but couldn't. The images had been so lifelike. His phone wouldn't work. And when he tried to call out for help, his voice wouldn't work. He felt so utterly helpless. He woke up with a start, sitting straight up in bed.

After falling back to sleep only to repeat the same horrible nightmare, he got out of bed and decided to start his day extra early. There was so much work to be done if he had any hope of harvesting enough grapes for winemaking. Of course, this year he would have to combine his grapes with some from another vineyard to make it worth his while.

He wasn't sure why he was putting in this much effort. He could have just sold the vineyard "as is," but it bothered him that his childhood home had fallen into such disrepair.

Underneath all of his excuses was guilt. It weighed heavy on him. For years, he'd been able to ignore it. Now that he was back at the Dupré Vineyard, it was impossible for him to get out from beneath the blanket of regrets.

He felt guilty that he'd left and not looked back after his grandmother's funeral. Of course, the choice hadn't been entirely his. His grandfather had played a large part in that decision, when he insisted he didn't need Antoine's help.

After a heated conversation, his grandfather had told him to get out and not come back. The words had hurt more than Antoine had expected them to. In the end, he'd heeded his grandfather's words.

And that was why when the estate's attorney contacted him to inform him that he'd inherited the estate, he'd been shocked. He'd been all set to turn around and sell it, but when he saw the place in poor condition, he'd felt compelled to fix up his childhood home and get the vineyard back up and running properly.

But he didn't want to think about the past.

He had enough in the present to keep his mind occupied, including the injured woman in the hospital.

When he took a break that morning, he phoned the hospital to see if the woman was still there. It was a little hard to check on her when he didn't know what name to give them when they asked. It took a bit, but he was finally put in touch with the fourth-floor nurses' station. They let him know that the woman was still there. They inquired if he wanted to speak with her. He declined and said he didn't want to disturb her.

He couldn't imagine what it would be like to wake up and not know where he was, how he'd gotten there and, most of all, not knowing his own name. Maybe there was a way he could help her.

After disconnecting the call to the hospital, he phoned the hotel where he'd crossed paths with the woman. He was a business acquaintance of the owner and was hoping he could shed some light on the woman's identity.

"Hey, Claude, I was wondering if you could help me," Antoine said.

"Sure. Anything. Do you need a suite for a night?"

"Something a little easier than that. I was

hoping you could tell me if one of your employees is missing."

"Missing? No. Does this have something to do with the woman that fell yesterday?"

"Yes, it does. I just thought since she was coming in the employee entrance that she might work at the hotel."

"I can understand what you're thinking and I had the same thought yesterday. So I checked and she doesn't work here."

"That's too bad."

"You sound like you're invested in the woman."

"No." The answer was a little too quick. "It's just that I feel bad for her. Would you know if she was a guest?"

"Not that I've heard. And if she was a guest, I don't see her using the back steps. However, we were conducting interviews for a housekeeper yesterday. Perhaps that's why she was here."

At last, he felt like they were getting somewhere. He knew the woman was going to need some work and money, so he asked, "Did you fill the position?"

"Afraid we did. Wish I could be of more help."

Too bad the position had been filled. That might have been really helpful to the woman.

Still, he felt if he told her about the house-keeping position that it might trigger a memory for her.

All of this talk of housekeepers had him thinking about the cleaning that needed to be done around the château. He definitely had to hire some help. Perhaps the mystery woman would be interested in the position when she recovered from her injuries. It would help her financially until she got her memory back and it would help him prepare the estate to be sold.

With that thought in mind, he showered and headed to the hospital. He was supposed to have an online conference call, but he called his assistant and had it rescheduled. His assistant wasn't too happy about it, but she did as he asked.

He stopped along the way to pick up a few toiletries for the woman. He didn't know what the hospital would supply or what she had in her suitcase, but he figured he better take her a few things. And so with the help of a salesclerk, he moved to the checkout with a toothbrush, toothpaste, a brush, a comb and a bunch of little bottles.

At the hospital, he made his way to Jeanne Dupont's room. It was the name they used for people without identities. On the way there he couldn't help but wonder if she'd had any glimmer of a memory. He wondered what her birth name was… Angeline? No. Michelle? She didn't strike him as a Michelle. Claire? Um… No.

By then he'd reached the mystery woman's room. He stepped up and rapped his knuckles lightly on the open door. She glanced up from a paperback she was reading.

Her eyes widened when she saw him. She lowered the book to her chest as a smile bloomed on her face. "You're back."

"I am." He found himself momentarily distracted as her smile lit up her whole face and made her eyes twinkle like fine gems. How had he missed how beautiful she was? She was really quite breathtaking.

Realizing that she'd caught him staring, he glanced away. "How are you doing?"

"Okay. The police were here and took a report about my stolen purse. I'm afraid I wasn't much help. They told me the chance of recovering it was slim. And since there were no cameras in that area, they don't have any leads on catching the thief."

"I'm sorry they weren't able to help."

She shrugged and then grimaced from pain. "Anyway, I'm hoping to get out of here today. I've been waiting to see the doctor. He was supposed to be in before lunch, but he got called away for an emergency. A nurse gave me a book she'd finished reading. It helps fill the time."

Antoine stepped up to the side of the bed and placed the bag on the small table. "I brought you a few things I thought you might need."

She reached for the bag and glanced inside. "Aww…thank you. When I have some money I'll pay you back, if you let me know where to send it."

He shook his head. "No need to worry about it." He was quite wealthy, but he didn't say that to her. Instead, he smiled and then said, "Consider it a gift of sorts."

Color filled her cheeks, making her look even more beautiful than just a moment ago. He didn't know that was possible because he thought she was stunning.

Realizing the direction of his thoughts, he attempted to rein them in by continuing their conversation. "And how's your memory? Were you able to recall anything?" He had to admit that he was curious to know more about her. He'd never known anyone to have amnesia.

She shook her head. "I still can't remember anything. I don't even know what I like to eat. The doctor said the amnesia likely won't be permanent and hopefully my memory will come back in time. I just hope it comes back soon."

He nodded in understanding, even though he had absolutely no idea what she must be going through. He could only imagine that it must be scary to not know who you were or where you belonged. And on top of it all, she had absolutely no money because her purse had been stolen.

"Thanks." Her voice was soft.

He took a seat in the chair near her bed. The room was stark, with white walls and a white tile floor. There were no pops of color. Nothing to cheer up the very antiseptic atmosphere. He should have brought her flowers or a stuffed animal, anything to lift her spirits.

"What will you do when you're released? Where will you go?" He was genuinely worried about her and that surprised him.

He hadn't let himself get close to anyone since his grandmother. She had been kind to him, but his grandfather was the opposite. He was a hard man to get to know and fiercely independent.

"I—I don't know." The woman toyed with the hem of the white blanket on her bed. "I was thinking of going back to the hotel where the accident happened and see if they know anything about me."

"I tried that."

She turned her head toward him, her eyes reflecting her surprise. "You did?"

"I know the owner."

"That's great." Her face lit up with hope. "What did he tell you?"

"I'm afraid not much. There were no employees missing and there were no missing guests."

"Oh." The hope drained from her face, leaving a look of sadness and confusion. She turned away and resumed nervously toying with the blanket. "Thank you for trying. I appreciate it."

He felt bad that he hadn't been able to do more to help. He racked his brain searching for an idea.

Knock-knock.

They both turned to the door. Antoine recognized the older man with short gray hair from yesterday. It was Dr. Tournet.

The doctor had a serious disposition, but when his gaze came to rest on the woman in the bed, he bestowed a friendly smile upon her. "And how are you doing today?"

She shrugged. "The same as yesterday."

He pulled a light from his pocket and

shined it in her eyes. As he examined her, he asked, "Have you had any memories come to you?"

"No."

"Hmm… You were brought in with a suitcase, weren't you?"

"Yes, but there's nothing in there with my identity. Just a bunch of clothes and shoes."

"I see. And did you recognize any of the items."

She shook her head. "They all felt strange to me."

"Strange, how?"

She shrugged. "I just had the feeling that I didn't normally dress that way. But that seems ridiculous, as there was nothing wrong with the clothing. There were jeans and T-shirts and some skirts as well as shorts. I don't know what it was about them that felt off. Maybe it's just me. I'm just so confused."

"It's okay. Give yourself some time to sort these things out."

"How long will this take?"

"It's hard to say. You took quite a blow to the face and head. Your memories may not come back at all, but in the majority of cases they do. The memories might come to you piece by piece, or they could all come back at once. I've seen it happen both ways. It's different for everyone."

"I just wish it would hurry up. I have no idea what I'm supposed to do next."

"I want you to see me next week. The nurse will give you the information. If you have any problems between now and then, come back to the hospital."

While they wrapped up things, Antoine told himself that none of this was his problem and yet it felt as though it was his problem. Maybe if he hadn't been distracted with his phone, he would have seen the thief and been able to stop him before he grabbed her purse.

He knew there was still no guarantee that he could have reached the man in time to stop him, but if he'd at least tried, he wouldn't feel so bad. Perhaps he could give her some money to help get her back on her feet.

He reached for his wallet. "I know you lost your purse during the incident, so I wanted to give you this." He withdrew all of the cash he had with him. When she didn't reach for it, he said, "Go ahead and take it. You don't have to worry about paying me back or anything."

Her gaze moved from him to the money and then back to him again. "Why would you give me money? You don't even know me."

He kept his hand outstretched. "I just feel bad that this happened to you."

"And yet you had nothing to do with it."

"Still, if I had been paying attention, I might have been able to stop him."

She pushed away his fist full of cash. "I don't want your money. None of this was your fault."

He was surprised and impressed in equal parts that she'd refused his handout. "But what will you do?"

There was a pause, as though she was trying to figure out a legitimate answer to his question. "I don't know."

"What if this was a loan? You can pay me back whenever you are back on your feet."

She hesitated. Then she nodded.

When he handed her the money, their fingertips touched. A tingling sensation raced up his arm. It settled in his chest. He chose to ignore the unfamiliar reaction.

She pulled her hand away. "Thank you. I'll pay you back as soon as I can."

"There's no rush." He paused when he realized that he still didn't know her name. "What should I call you? I don't think you want to go around known as Jeanne Dupont, do you?"

She shook her head. "It's just a constant reminder of all I've lost."

"So what name would you like to go by?"

"I don't know. I've haven't thought about it."

"This is your chance to go by any name of your choosing. So what shall it be? Noémie?"

She shook her head.

"Éléanor? Chloé? Léna? Violette?"

With each name he mentioned, she shook her head. "None of them feel like me."

He was running out of name suggestions. He supposed he could pull out his phone and search for names, but first he said, "What name does feel like you?"

Her eyebrows drew together as though she was giving the question great thought. The silence dragged on. And then she said, "Cherie."

Anticipation bubbled up inside him. Maybe at last her memory was starting to come back to her. "Does it mean something to you?"

"No."

His hope felt like a balloon that had just been pricked with a pin. "Oh. Then how did you come up with it?"

"It was the name of the first nurse that helped me in the emergency department. And I hope when my memory comes back to me that I'm as kind and caring as she is."

He smiled. "That's a great choice."

He sat there thinking that there was no way he could just walk away. It wasn't like him to be the overprotective type. But there was this vulnerability to Cherie and she hid it behind a tough exterior.

Even though he had his own problems to focus on—like keeping his family's vineyard, or selling it "as is"—he had to find a way to help her. He just had to give it some more thought.

If the past was lost to her, she had to figure out who she was going to be right now.

It was hard to do when she knew nothing about herself. Surely there had to be some clue to who she was and what she was doing in Saint-Tropez.

"If I had a suitcase with me, it must mean I was here on holiday." Cherie gave the idea some more thought, hoping it would trigger a memory.

"Or you just moved here."

"Oh. That's a possibility. And perhaps I was planning to stay at the hotel until I found a place to live."

"But you were coming up the back steps, which is usually used by the staff."

"I was?"

"Yes. When I was talking to my friend at the

hotel, he mentioned that they were conducting interviews for housekeeping that day. It's possible you were there for an interview."

The thought of landing a job sent a sense of urgency through her. "Are they still interviewing?"

"I'm afraid not." He was quiet for a moment as though giving her lack of employment some thought. "But I'm looking to hire. Although I'm not sure you'd want to take the position."

He'd already done so much for her. She wasn't sure she should take him up on the offer, but in her dire circumstances, she needed to at least hear him out. "What sort of position would it be?"

"I need a housekeeper for my family's château. I should have hired someone already, but I just haven't taken the time."

A housekeeper? It didn't sound so hard. If she'd been a housekeeper in the past, maybe the job would help jar her memory.

"So you just want me to clean for you?"

"Yes, and perhaps some light cooking. It doesn't have to be anything fancy."

Cooking? She couldn't recall if she could cook. She supposed she would find out soon enough. "Where is your château?"

"Not far from here, so you would still be close to town."

The offer was tempting. It would give her a chance to pay him back for his generosity. "If I were to take you up on the offer, it would only be temporary until I figure out who I am."

"Of course, but perhaps I need to explain that the château hasn't been looked after in quite a while. And it'll take a lot of work to make it habitable again. It might be more of a challenge than you're looking for."

She was confused. "You don't live there?"

"No. Well…yes."

"So which is it?"

"No, I don't normally live there, but right now I am staying there. And there's a small cottage on the grounds that you could use."

"Oh." She liked the thought of having a roof over her head. She had nowhere else to go right now—at least that she could remember. "But I couldn't pay you rent."

"No worries. If you come work for me, room and board will be included."

"And if I don't take the job?" She'd be crazy not to take it, but she was still weighing her options.

"The cottage will still be available to you if you like."

She glanced at him to make sure he was serious. From the expression on his face, she surmised his offer was genuine. Was he really as good as he seemed? There was so much she didn't know about him.

"So, Cherie, while we wait for your official discharge, you might want to put on some of those clothes in your suitcase." He gestured to the suitcase sitting in the corner of the room. "And then you'll be ready to go home, um... to the château."

"You don't have to do that."

"I know. I want to."

"In that case, I'll take you up on the offer." She scrambled out of bed and headed for the suitcase.

Once she'd settled on an outfit, she turned toward the bathroom.

"Cherie?" He spoke louder. "Cherie?"

Suddenly realizing he was speaking to her, she turned around. "Sorry. I forgot my new name."

"You'll get used to it. I just wanted to tell you that you forgot your toiletries."

"Oh, yes." Heat warmed her cheeks. She rushed over and grabbed the bag. "Thank you, again." And then she slipped into the bathroom.

Why was Antoine being so kind to her?

She knew she wasn't in a position to question his generosity, but she was determined to do good work for him. It was the least she could do after all he'd done for her.

CHAPTER FOUR

SHE HAD A name now.

Cherie let the name roll around in her mind for a moment. Yes, she was comfortable with it. And she would never forget the original Cherie from the hospital. The friendly nurse had calmed her when she'd started to panic over her amnesia. She'd assured her that everything would work out.

And though Cherie wasn't her real name, she couldn't be known as "that woman" or "hey, you" forever. Plus, it was a nice name—a fun name. She could use a bit of happiness right now.

She glanced to the side at Antoine as he sat in the driver's seat of his low-slung red-and-black sports car. He looked comfortable behind the steering wheel as he maneuvered them through the city traffic.

From his stylish clothes to his designer watch, he didn't appear to have money problems. Something told her they didn't come from the same walk of life. The clothes in her suitcase indicated her life was a lot less glamorous. While it appeared he didn't have to work for a living, she must have had a job—if only she knew what it might be.

As they headed toward the countryside, a peaceful silence settled over the car. She appreciated how Antoine was working so hard to make her comfortable. He had no obligation to help her out and yet he'd gone out of his way for her. Not everyone would be so generous.

If only she could remember who she was, she wouldn't feel like a burden. She wondered about her life. Was she an orphan, or perhaps from a big family? Was there someone out there that loved and missed her?

"What are you thinking about?" Antoine's voice interrupted her thoughts.

"I was wondering if there's anyone in this world that misses me." For a moment, she felt so alone.

Antoine's hand reached over and covered hers. His long fingers gave her hand a squeeze. "You'll see them again."

"I hope so." She wasn't even sure whom she was missing. "But what if I don't get my memory back? What if I never remember my name?"

"The doctor said it could take some time. You took a big hit to the head. Just relax and the memories will come to you."

"How can you be so sure?"

"Because when I'm struggling to remember some obscure fact at the office, I'll strain my brain and get nothing. But as soon as I relax and think about something else, the answer will come to me."

"And you think it works the same with amnesia?" She wanted to think it was that simple, but it'd already been more than twenty-four hours and she still hadn't recalled the slightest detail about her life before the fall.

He put his hand on the gearshift as he slowed down for an intersection. "I don't know, but I'd like to think so."

She couldn't stop thinking about what her life might be like. Was she a famous actress? Probably not. No one in the hospital recognized her. But after looking in the mirror and seeing her two black eyes and bandaged nose, her own mother likely wouldn't recognize her.

And then there were the clothes in her suitcase. They were nothing special. Still, if she was looking for a job in Saint-Tropez, this must be her home now. She looked at her fingers. There were no marks on them, as though she normally wore rings, so it was doubtful that she was married or had a fiancé.

"Do you think I work around here?" She glanced around at the colorful shops.

"I'm not so sure. If you do, why would you have had a suitcase with you?"

He was right. She'd forgotten about that. Right now, she seemed to be forgetting everything—except his piercing eyes that made her feel as though he could see straight through her. But what did he see when he looked at her?

Did he see someone he found attractive? Her heart leaped at the thought. Or did he see her as someone he felt sorry for? She didn't want him helping her out of pity.

She pushed aside the unsettling thoughts. She had to focus on finding answers to her past. It was the only way she would find her way home and feel whole again.

Maybe Antoine was right. Maybe she was too focused on her past. Maybe she needed to think about something else.

Her gaze shifted to Antoine. She longed to know more about him. "Where do you live when you're not at the château?"

"I have an apartment in Paris."

"How long are you going to be in Saint-Tropez?" She was thankful that she'd remembered their location. Her short-term memory seemed to be fully intact. It just left her long-term memory that needed to recover.

He paused as though giving her question some thought. "I'm not sure."

"How many people work at the château?"

"Around a dozen people work in the fields."

She didn't know anything about châteaus, so she didn't know if that was a large staff or not. As they continued their drive to his château, she peppered him with questions. There was just something about his dark good looks and his quietness that made her want to draw back the curtains and learn about the man that he kept hidden from the world.

What was he really like? Why was this château so important to him? And why was he willing to help her? Was he attracted to her? The thought made her heart pitter-patter. She cast him a sideways glance. He was definitely very handsome. And then she remembered her black-and-blue face. No one could be attracted to her when she looked like such a mess.

The car slowed down and turned. "We're here."

She read the sign at the end of the drive: Château Escoffier Dupré.

All around them were rows of grapevines. They looked green and healthy. As they neared the château, she noticed a difference. Toward the back of the estate, the vines were overgrown. The château had a small yard around it but it too needed attention.

She focused on the château. If she looked past its need for a fresh coat of paint, she saw that it had good bones. It was much larger than she'd been expecting. Why would someone let a beautiful place like this fall into disrepair?

It was on the tip of her tongue to ask Antoine, but she held back the words. She'd already pushed him enough with her questions. She sensed he wasn't used to talking about himself because he only ever answered her question and never offered anything more.

"This is so much larger than I was expecting," she said.

He pulled the car to a stop in front of the château. "Well, this is home for now."

They both got out of the car. She stared up at the three-story château with four turrets in each corner. It was impressive in size.

"It looks like a palace," she said.

"A palace?" He glanced from her to the château and back again. "It's been called a lot of things before but never a palace. I don't think it's nearly as elaborate."

"Perhaps not. I wouldn't know. But it's still quite impressive."

"I'm glad you think so since you'll be in charge of cleaning it."

Her mouth gaped. "You want me to clean all of that?" When he nodded, she asked, "How many bedrooms does it have? A hundred?"

He chuckled. "There are eight bedrooms on the second floor. There are more on the third floor, but I haven't been up there since I was a boy."

She swallowed hard. "And you want me to clean all of it?"

"That was the idea. Unless you're having reservations."

She knew he'd mentioned a château with grounds, but this place was even larger than she'd been imagining. But she refused to let it intimidate her. "No. I can do this."

Antoine moved to the trunk to retrieve her suitcase. She followed him. And then they reached for the suitcase at the same time.

Their fingers touched. His hand was warm and softer than she would have imagined. Time seemed to stand still as their fingers continued to touch. She lifted her gaze to meet his.

She was going to say something, but as he stared back at her, the words vanished. Her thoughts halted. The only thing she could hear at that moment was the pounding of her heart.

And when his gaze momentarily dipped to her lips, the breath caught in her lungs. Was he thinking of kissing her? Her pulse sped up.

Suddenly, there was nothing she wanted more than to feel his lips pressed to hers. Was he leaning closer to her? Or was she leaning into him? Did it even matter? The only thing she cared about right now was finding out what it was like to kiss him.

Just then, the sound of a machine grew louder as it rumbled along. The unexpected moment ended as quickly as it had started. Was it a moment? She questioned what had just happened. Was it possible it was all a part of her imagination?

They both turned to find a smallish excavator headed toward them. It bounced its way over the gravel and came to a stop not far from them.

"Before we get you settled, I need to have a word with José." He moved toward the excavator.

Cherie didn't know where to go and so she

stood there, feeling awkward. It shouldn't be like this. Frustration churned within her. She should know where she belonged and her real name. Instead, she was left in the dark.

When Antoine glanced her way, his gaze met hers. Her worries moved to the back of her mind. She knew she shouldn't stare but her body refused to move. She was drawn to this sexy, charming man in a way she'd never been attracted to anyone else—at least she didn't think so.

With her heart beating fast, she lowered her gaze. She couldn't be certain, but surely she wouldn't have such a strong reaction to Antoine if she was involved, heart and soul, with another man.

She lifted her gaze to meet his once more. Her stomach dipped. The way he looked at her made her feel like she was the only woman in the world.

Heat gathered in her chest and rushed to her cheeks. As sexy as she found him, she couldn't afford to complicate this arrangement. Until her memory returned, she had to protect her job, which included room and board. She didn't have a backup plan.

She glanced away. She needed to stay focused on regaining her memory, not let herself get distracted with the way his stare made her heart flutter.

CHAPTER FIVE

HE'D ALMOST KISSED HER.

He'd wanted to experience one of Cherie's sweet kisses.

Antoine was drawn to her. When he looked at her, he didn't see her injuries. He saw a strong woman, who didn't let life's setbacks stop her. He saw a woman who didn't want anything from him. She didn't place any expectations upon him.

Antoine swallowed hard. What was wrong with him? He was never like that with women. In fact, he hadn't dated in months. Maybe that was part of his problem.

Ever since he'd been alerted of his grandfather's sudden death and the fact that he was the sole heir, his thoughts had been on preparing the estate for sale. This place was filled with memories, not all of them good. It was time to close the door on his past.

As such, for the past two months he'd been

living in the guesthouse instead of the main house. It was so much easier because he didn't have any memories attached to the place. But he couldn't stay there any longer.

He came to a stop outside of the guesthouse and turned to her. "I'm sorry the place is a mess. I didn't know you would be staying here or I would have cleaned up."

"Oh. That's okay." She sent him a smile that ignited a funny feeling in his chest. "After all, I'm here to do the cleaning."

He opened the door and let her enter ahead of him. Once she was inside, he moved into the bedroom. He gathered his discarded clothes from the armchair.

He wasn't normally a messy person. He liked his surroundings neat and orderly. However, since he had been at the estate, he'd been spending night and day out in the vineyard when he wasn't meeting with local establishments to line up sales for that year's wine.

He turned and stripped the bed. He bunched the sheets up into a ball. They'd have to go to the main house to be laundered.

"You don't have to do that," Cherie said from behind him.

He pulled off the pillowcases. "You just got out of the hospital. You shouldn't be doing housework."

"But I feel better." She sent him a brief smile.

He wasn't so sure he believed her. He moved to the closet and withdrew a fresh set of linens. This was something he'd never done for any woman, but there was something special about Cherie. She made him want to go out of his way for her.

He turned back toward the bed and had to stop short to keep from running into Cherie. She held her hands out to him as though to take the linens from him. He hesitated.

"At least let me help you."

And so together, they made the bed. He'd never done this with anyone but his grandmother. She'd believed that no one should be pampered. She insisted Antoine learn how to take care of himself.

Even though when he was young they'd had a household staff, he'd learned to do the basics, from laundry to cooking. It was never anything fancy, but he could do some simple cooking. It all seemed like a lifetime ago.

His grandfather's family had been wealthy, and the vineyard had been passed down through the generations. His grandfather had done his best, but as Antoine had recently learned by going through the vineyard's financials, his grandfather hadn't been good with money. The accounts had all been drained from one bad investment after another.

Luckily Antoine hadn't taken after his grandfather in that respect. He'd started working at the vineyard as a kid. His grandfather paid him and Antoine saved every cent.

He continued to work through school and university. By the time he'd earned his business degree, he was set to start his own business.

Of course, his initial endeavor into the business world had been small. Over the years his import-export business had grown. He found he had an ability to sell people most anything. He focused primarily on electronics.

"That's much better." Cherie's voice drew him from his thoughts.

He glanced at the bed. Not too bad. It might have even passed his grandmother's inspection. "There's some food and drinks in the fridge. Help yourself to them." He gathered his toiletries from the bathroom and put them in his bag. "Is there anything else I can get you?"

"Uh, no. Thank you. If you'll show me where you want me to start cleaning, I can get started."

He shook his head. "Not today. You need to rest."

"Are you sure? I don't mind working today."

"Doctor's orders. Remember?" He gathered the dirty laundry in one arm and grabbed his bag with the other. "If you need anything, call me."

"But I don't have your number and I don't have my phone anymore."

He frowned. "I won't be far. I'll be in the fields today. I'll have someone check on you every now and then. If you need anything, just let them know."

He hesitated. Should he do something else? His mind raced. He wasn't used to playing host. And as much as he wanted to find an excuse to stay, it was best that he put some distance between them. He turned and headed for the door.

"So I'll see you later?"

Was there a note of hopefulness in her voice? Or was that a bit of wishful thinking on his part? "Um, sure. I'll see you at dinnertime." He started outside and then turned back. "What would you like to eat?"

"You don't have to cook for me."

"I'm not."

"Oh." Color bloomed in her cheeks. "I'm

sorry. I misunderstood. Would you like me to cook something?"

He shook his head. "I can pick up something in the village. I just need to know what sounds good to you."

"Pizza."

"Pizza?" When she nodded, he asked, "What kind?"

She thought for a moment. "La Reine."

He liked her tastes. He always enjoyed a pizza with lots of tomato sauce, extra mozzarella cheese, ham, mushrooms and olives. He would have to get a large one so there'd be leftovers. "You've got it. I'll see you later."

This time he made his way out the door. And when he thought of turning around one last time, he heard the snick of the door closing. He kept on moving.

He wasn't quite sure how the day had gone from him wanting to check in on Cherie at the hospital to him bringing her home and giving her his bed. And now they were having dinner together. He knew it wasn't a date, so why was he letting it get to him?

She couldn't just lie around.

Cherie got straight to work. She washed the dishes in the small kitchenette and then proceeded to straighten a few things here and there. With the guesthouse in order, she perused the fridge at noon and selected some bread, cheese and fruit.

As she ate lunch, she wondered what Antoine was doing. Was he staying away from the guesthouse because she was there? Or was he skipping lunch altogether because he'd spent so much time with her that he was behind in his work?

She felt bad for disrupting his life. She was determined to do everything she could to repay him for his generosity.

After lunch, she went for a walk around the grounds. The estate appeared to have been neglected for some time. Bushes were overgrown. Gardens had been taken over by the weeds. But it was nothing that couldn't be righted with some time and hard work.

She turned to the enormous château. She wanted to step up to the giant front doors and have a peek inside, but she didn't want to intrude. Soon enough, she'd see the work that awaited her. It would no doubt be as challenging as the outside.

But by that afternoon, her head hurt. Sleep had been difficult in the hospital. Between her fervent effort to regain her memories, the noises in the hall and the unfamiliar surroundings, she'd only gotten a bit of sleep here and there. Maybe she should slow down—but just for today.

Tomorrow she'd start on the main house.

After a couple of pain relievers and lying down for a bit, her headache eased. By then it was nearing dinnertime. She had no idea what time Antoine would arrive, but she had the kitchen table cleaned off and ready for dinner.

Unless he preferred to eat outside. She hadn't thought of that before. There was a small balcony off the back of the guesthouse. It had the most magnificent view of the vineyard. And it was less cozy than eating inside.

Oh, yes, they should dine outdoors. There was less chance of them getting lost in each other's eyes. They'd be too busy taking in the beautiful scenery.

The more she thought about it, the more certain she was that it's where they should dine. She made her way onto the deck to find a white bistro-style table and chairs. They were totally darling.

However, it appeared that it had been a long time since they'd seen any TLC. The white metal had a fine layer of dirt over the tabletop and the chairs. Cobwebs lined the underside of the table. It was nothing she couldn't clean up.

And so she set to work. In a closet just off the kitchen, she found an old broom. She swept the balcony and cleared the cobwebs. She cleaned the table and chairs with all of their intricate-cut floral design.

"There you are." Antoine's voice came from behind her.

She finished wiping off the back of one chair and then straightened. She put a smile on her face and turned. She found him standing there with a pizza in one hand and a bag of groceries in the other. "I thought we could have dinner out here."

He glanced around at the balcony. "Looks like you've been busy."

While he was checking out the balcony, she was busy checking him out. It appeared he hadn't just grabbed a pizza on his way home from the field. First, he'd taken time to shower and put on fresh clothes. He looked good. Real good.

Refusing to let on that his presence got to her, she casually shrugged. "It wasn't that much. Let me just wash my hands and grab us some plates."

She moved toward the door. It wasn't until she was already in motion that she realized she had to cross in front of him in order to get to the door. Their bodies practically had to touch.

"Excuse me." Her heart leaped to her throat. He was so temptingly close.

If she stopped right here and tilted her chin upward, she wondered if he would kiss her. The thought teased her mind, but she refused to give in to her desires. With concerted effort, she kept moving.

Once inside the kitchen, she blew out a pent-up breath. What was wrong with her? It had to be the bump on the head. That's why Antoine was getting to her. If she'd just give it some time, the initial attraction would pass.

He followed her inside and proceeded to put the food he'd brought in the fridge. She was curious to know what he'd bought, but she resisted getting that close to him again.

Instead, she washed her hands and then grabbed the plates. She refused to let her out-of-control hormones ruin the evening. She just needed to concentrate on learning more about her new job. With her mind distracted, she wouldn't have time to notice the way his top shirt buttons were undone, giving the slightest glimpse of his muscled chest. She inwardly groaned. She was in a lot of trouble.

As she headed out the door, he was coming in. "I'm just going to grab us something to drink."

"Oh. Okay." She continued out to the table that suddenly seemed so much smaller.

Somehow she managed to make small talk as they ate most of the pizza. It was just so good that one or two pieces just wasn't enough. And she hadn't eaten very much in the hospital.

As they sat there sipping their wine, the sun hovered on the horizon. It splashed brilliant shades of pink and purple over the puffy clouds. It was a beautiful evening.

She glanced over at Antoine in order to say something about the view, but when she looked his way, he was already staring back at her. Her pulse raced.

She was the first to look away. "This is really good wine."

"It was the vineyard's signature wine. I'm hoping that one day soon it will be the vineyard's top seller again."

"Is that why you're working so hard in the fields?"

He turned his chair to stare out at the colorful sunset. "Yes. When I sell the place, I want it to be a functioning vineyard. There are years of neglect that we're trying to overcome."

"You're selling this place. But why?" And then she realized how forward that sounded. She rushed on. "I mean, it's so beautiful here. If it was my place I couldn't imagine parting with it."

He stretched out his legs and crossed them at the ankles. "I have another life in Paris. I can't keep both my business and the vineyard. One would always suffer while my attention was on the other."

"What type of business?"

"It's an import-export business. Our primary focus is electronics."

"Huh."

"What does *huh* mean?"

"It's just that electronics is quite different from wine. Why don't you hire a manager to handle the vineyard in your absence?"

He shook his head. "I'm not keeping the vineyard that long."

"Oh. I thought you were. With all of the hard work you're putting into the place, I thought you were holding on to it in order to start a family."

He frowned and shook his head again. "That's not going to happen."

If he was so insistent on selling the estate, why not sell the place as it was? She longed to ask him, but she got the feeling if she pushed him any further, he'd totally shut down. And she didn't want that to happen.

She swished the wine around in her glass. "So you're having me clean the château in order to sell it?"

"Something like that." He swallowed the last of his wine.

"I'm sorry you have to choose. Giving up this place must be really hard for you."

"Not as hard as you might think." He got to his feet. "I should be going. I have work awaiting me and you need your rest. Speaking of which, there's no need for you to work tomorrow."

"Yes, there is."

His eyebrows rose. "You really want to work tomorrow?"

She nodded. "It's better than sitting around rattling my brain and coming up with no answers about my past. You have no idea how frustrating it can be."

"I understand. Not really. But you know what I mean." He picked up his plate and the pizza box.

She rushed to stand up. "You don't have to clean up. I've got it."

"I insist."

"It's really no problem. I owe you so much for this opportunity."

His gaze met hers. "I didn't do much. It's you who is helping me get this place ready for photos so I can have my real-estate agent list it."

"I... I'm happy to help in any way I can." It's the least she owed him after the way he made sure she had a roof over her head and gave her a job. He was like her fairy godfather. The thought of this serious businessman being a fairy made her laugh.

His eyebrows drew together. "What's so funny?"

"Oh. Uh... Nothing." There was no way she was admitting to thinking of him with a sparkly light blue suit, wings and a wand. The smile continued to pull at her lips. "I just can't believe all of this has happened and you were there to help me. Thank you."

He hesitated as though he wasn't so sure he believed her. "You're welcome."

She led the way into the house. Together they cleaned the dishes and put them away. He left the remaining pizza for her and she didn't complain. It was definitely her favorite. And the thought made her happy because she had learned something about herself.

Antoine made her happy, too. He was a bit on the quiet side, but maybe that was because he'd been spending too much time alone on this great big estate. But things were different now. She was here to keep him company.

If only she wasn't tempted to kiss him each time she saw him. Maybe a good night's sleep would help clear her thoughts. After all, she couldn't afford to throw herself at him. She needed to keep this job with all of its perks... at least until her memory returned.

CHAPTER SIX

TODAY WAS THE first full day of her new life.

Her new name was Cherie.

And she was the housekeeper for Antoine Dupré.

It all felt so strange to her and, dare she admit it, a little exciting. She was on an exploration to learn about herself. But in the end, she wondered if she would like the person she'd been before the accident. She hoped so.

Cherie yawned and stretched. She hadn't fallen asleep until late. Her mind had been filled with the awkward moment when they'd almost kissed. If that excavator hadn't come along when it did, would he have kissed her?

Her heart raced every time she recalled the moment. She didn't have to wonder if she would have kissed him back. She instinctively knew the answer. Oh, yes, she would have.

And then there had been that moment on the balcony. Was it a moment? Had his thoughts gone in the same direction as hers? She had no idea. She'd refused to meet his gaze because if she had—if she had lifted her chin, she might have given in to her desires and kissed him.

She longed to know what his mouth would feel like against her lips. She wondered what the big draw was to him. Sure, he was great-looking, but she couldn't help but wonder if it was something more.

Not that she would ever find out because she had a job to do and hopefully one morning very soon she would wake up with her full memory totally intact. And then she'd be gone—back to her old life.

She missed her other life, which was really weird considering she knew absolutely nothing about it. She'd like to think that she had family who cared about her. She hoped that it was a good life.

But even if her life wasn't so great, once she had her memory back, she would know and understand herself...as well as anyone understands themselves. She longed to know what food she liked to eat, what her favorite color was and most especially her real name.

She didn't have time to contemplate any of that at the moment because she'd set her alarm to go off early. She didn't want to appear lazy or unappreciative of what Antoine had done for her. Without him, she'd be homeless on the street without a cent to her name.

She wanted to show him how much she appreciated this opportunity, but she kept wondering what she'd gotten herself into. The château was far from small and cozy. It was big and massive.

Showered and dressed, she looked in the mirror at the bruises, scrapes and stitches. She was an utter mess. Without the bandage, she at least didn't resemble a mummy.

She gingerly fingered the bridge of her nose. It appeared to be almost twice the size it normally would be. The slightest touch made her wince. There wasn't a chance she'd be wearing makeup anytime soon.

She turned her back to the mirror. She moved to the kitchenette and was touched that Antoine had insisted on stocking the fridge for her. At that moment, her stomach shivered with nerves. Maybe she'd eat something later.

She let herself outside and found the sun shining bright. The birds were chirping on the warm morning. In the distance, she could hear machinery humming along. Antoine must be hard at work. She felt even worse about sleeping in.

She made her way up the steps to the large

double doors. They were painted black with brass fixtures. She was about to knock when she realized that with Antoine working in the vineyard, there would be no one there to answer. In fact, if she was to be the house-keeper, she would be the one answering the door, right?

And so she let herself inside. She wasn't sure what she expected but it wasn't what she found. There was heavy dust everywhere. And cobwebs. She cringed. It would appear she didn't like spiders, but who could blame her?

However, when she looked past the obvi-ous neglect, she could see what the place had once been. It had been impressive not only in size but also style. Beneath the filth on the floor were black-and-white tiles in a dia-mond pattern.

A mural of the vineyard was painted on one entire wall. She approached it to have a closer look. It was very detailed and color-ful. She would have to be quite careful when she cleaned it.

The remainder of the foyer was done in a creamy white and there was a small fountain in the corner. She wondered if it still worked. She couldn't wait to find out.

She craned her neck to look upward. It was

a really high ceiling. It would take a tall ladder to get up there to clean. The thought made her uncomfortable. She got the feeling she was afraid of heights. That could be a problem in a château of this size.

As she peered upward, she took in the four white crisscross ceiling beams that surrounded decorative plasterwork. Another area that wouldn't be easy to clean. Each swirl and dip would have to be hand-cleaned for fear of crumbling the aged plaster. She would have to speak with Antoine about having a professional come in. They would be able to give the ceiling a professional clean and fix the small cracks.

She walked around the downstairs. Other than the kitchen, the rest of the first floor didn't look as though it had been lived in for quite a while. The living room was huge and formal. The dining room was much the same.

There was a den in the back of the house that looked to have been used recently. There wasn't much dust in the room. She stopped in the middle of the room and turned, taking in the deep maroon couch with two bed pillows at one end. The couch rested in front of built-in bookcases loaded with hardback books.

Her attention returned to the couch. There was a cream-and-blue-colored quilt draped over the back of it. She wondered if Antoine or perhaps his grandfather had been living in this room. And if so, why?

As the question swirled through her mind, she moved on. She located a small bedroom just off the kitchen. The décor was minimal. A small dresser sat in the corner and beneath a window was a twin bed. Perhaps it was for the hired help. She wasn't sure.

She circled around to the foyer. She started up the sweeping staircase with the intricately carved banister. She felt as though she was walking through a museum. She couldn't even guess the great value of the artwork adorning the walls. Why would anyone let this place fall into disrepair?

The château looked as though it was just waiting for someone to breathe new life into it. She supposed she was that person, but she hoped Antoine knew this place was going to need so much more help than she could give it, from the plaster repair to restoring some of the fine artwork.

On the top floor, she found many small bedrooms. There was nothing special about them. In fact as fancy as the first floor had been, this floor was the complete opposite. And with the windows closed and the sun shining bright, it was quite stuffy with a musty scent.

This was a good place to start. She moved to the window in the first room and attempted to open it. It was stuck. She moved on to the next window. It opened. She kept going until she'd opened as many windows on the top floor that would open. At last, there was a breeze moving through the upstairs.

She sneezed. It hurt. A lot.

And then she sneezed again. The breeze had stirred up the dust. And sneezing was making her broken nose throb. It would appear she'd forgotten she had some allergies. She rushed around to close the windows. Airing the place out would have to wait.

"Cherie?" Antoine's voice echoed up the staircase. "Cherie, where are you?"

"Up here!"

She wasn't sure she was ready to see Antoine just yet. She told herself that her nervousness stemmed from the fact she hadn't even started to clean yet. In fact, she'd yet to find the cleaning stuff. And her anxiousness had absolutely nothing to do with fantasizing about him kissing her.

She ran her fingers over her short hair, hoping the breeze hadn't messed it up. And then she regretted not putting on some of the new makeup she found in the bag of toiletries Antoine had brought her in the hospital. Maybe she could have added some makeup under her eyes and on the large bruise on her cheek. But it was too late to worry about her appearance now.

Antoine climbed to the top of the steps. "There you are." He didn't smile but he didn't frown, either. "What are you doing up here?"

She shrugged. "I was just looking around. And it was so hot and stuffy up here that I opened the windows or rather the windows that I could get to open. Some of them are stuck."

He glanced around. "Are they all stuck?"

"No. I found out I have allergies and closed them again."

He nodded in understanding. "Make a note of the windows that aren't working and I'll bring someone in to fix them."

She breathed a little easier. "That's so good to know."

"What? Surely you didn't think I'd expect you to do everything on your own."

She shrugged. "I didn't know. This place is so big."

"You just tell me what help you need and I'll see that you get it."

She took the opportunity to mention the high ceilings that she would need assistance with as well as the cracked plaster and the artwork that needed some restoration.

"I'll have my assistant make some calls. My goal is to have this place cleaned and ready to sell in a month."

"A month?" That was a lot of work to do in just a month.

He arched an eyebrow. "Will that be a problem?"

"Um… No. I'll get to work." And then she realized her next problem. "Do you happen to know where I can find the cleaning supplies?"

He frowned as though giving it some thought. "Actually, I don't. Have a look around and if you can't find what you're looking for, let me know."

"Okay. Thanks."

"Why are you starting to work up here?" His pointed gaze searched hers.

Her first day and she was already making mistakes. Perhaps starting at the top and working her way down hadn't been the right decision. The truth was that she didn't have a clue what she was doing.

She swallowed hard. "I wasn't starting up here. I was having a look around." When his expression didn't change, she said, "You know, to have an idea of what needs to be done."

"Then why were you opening the windows?"

"Because it is quite musty up here. And if I'm expected to work up here, I don't want to be overwhelmed by the stink."

His eyebrows briefly rose. "I see. Okay. Just make sure you remember to close any windows you open at the end of the day."

"Yes, sir."

He frowned. "Why did you say that?"

"Say what? 'Yes, sir?'"

"Yes, that. You don't have to call me 'sir.'"

"What am I supposed to call you?"

"My name, Antoine. People at the office call me 'sir.' People helping in the vineyard call me 'sir.' I don't want to come home and have you call me 'sir,' too."

This time she was the one to arch an eyebrow. "But isn't that what one calls their boss?"

"I'm not your boss. I'm…"

Her words were hesitant. "My friend?"

His gaze met hers. He didn't say anything. Her stomach clenched. Had she overstepped? Assumed too much?

He glanced away. "Why don't I help you find the cleaning supplies? I suggest we start in the kitchen." He didn't wait for her response as he turned and headed back down the stairs.

She followed him, all the while wondering about the man in front of her. He was a mystery she wanted to solve.

Why had he insisted she not call him "sir"?

Did he want them to have a closer relationship?

Antoine searched through the many cabinets in the large kitchen, and he kept thinking about Cherie. There was something about her that he couldn't get out of his mind.

Even last night, when he was supposed to be sleeping, he'd been thinking of her and wondering if she was comfortable in the guest cottage. She'd slept in what had been his bed. The thought of them sharing something so intimate made her feel like less of a stranger.

Not sure where to stay in the musty place, he'd ended up in his old bedroom, surrounded by his childhood possessions. He was surprised to find the room had remained exactly as he had left it.

He'd thought for sure that his grandfather would have thrown out all of his stuff as soon as he'd walked out the door for good. Why had his grandfather kept those things? He supposed he would never know the answer to that question.

"Did you find anything?" Cherie's voice drew him from his thoughts.

"Uh...no. But I know there have to be supplies. Trust me, when I was a kid my grandmother insisted on a clean house. She even helped the housekeepers."

"So when you were a kid this place must have been amazing."

"It depends on what you mean by amazing. From the outside looking in, the house was immaculate." He stopped himself. He didn't want to open the door to his complicated past.

He never thought about it when he was in Paris. When he was in the city, his focus was on his import-export business. There were schedules to meet and deals to be made. His messy family history was the furthest thing from his mind.

And that's why he'd finally decided to sell this place. It might have been in his family for generations, but that didn't mean he wanted to deal with the memories at every turn. Besides, he didn't plan to marry. There would be no heirs to hand down the estate.

He refused to go through the worry and agony of losing someone he loved, the way his mother had died in childbirth. She had been so young. She should have been able to get through it, but she'd died right after he was born. She'd never even been able to hold him.

His grandmother had tried to fill the empty spot in his life, but as he got older, he'd pushed her away. He grew resentful of his grandfather's sternness and rebelled. And yet his grandmother was always there telling him that she loved him and that she refused to lose him, too. Grand had been the best. He wished she'd lived long enough to see him now as a successful international entrepreneur. He wished he'd told her how much he'd loved her.

A hand on his arm jarred him from his thoughts. He turned his head to Cherie. Concern filled her eyes. It was the same way his grandmother used to look at him when she worried about him.

"I'm sorry if I dredged up bad memories for you." Cherie's voice was soothing as she drew closer to him.

"It's not you. It's this place."

Her hand remained on his forearm. "I'm sorry." When he didn't respond, she said, "I'll start cleaning in the kitchen."

His gaze searched hers. "You don't have to start already. Rest. Recover."

"I don't want to sit around. I'll just get more frustrated when I can't remember anything from my past. It seems you and I have opposite problems."

"How's that?"

"You want to forget your past and I desperately want to remember mine."

"I'm sorry for focusing on my problems when yours are so much worse. I still believe you'll get your memory back."

His gaze lowered to her pink lips. They weren't painted with lipstick or gloss. They were bare and just begging for him to sample their sweetness. And yet he hesitated.

He didn't know if she felt the same way. However, the way she continued to stare back at him made his heart beat faster. As though she read his thoughts, she leaned forward. Her lips touched his. The breath hitched in the back of his throat.

So it wasn't just him that felt this intensity coursing between them. He wrapped his arms around her waist and pulled her close. As the kiss deepened, her arms slipped around his neck. Her fingernails scraped over his scalp, sending a cascade of sensations throughout his body. A moan swelled in the back of his throat.

He'd never felt this way with any other

woman. There was something special about Cherie—something that had him wishing she would never get her memory back.

As soon as he realized the direction of his thoughts, he pulled back. What was he thinking? He couldn't wish something like that on Cherie. It wasn't fair to her. She had a family out there and she needed to find them.

Even though she wasn't wearing any rings, she could have a boyfriend. The thought left a sour feeling in the pit of his stomach. He shouldn't have kissed her back, even if it felt good. So very good that he wanted to kiss her again.

He gave himself a mental shake, hoping to clarify his thoughts. "I'm sorry. That shouldn't have happened."

As she continued to stare at him with a pained look, she said, "You have nothing to apologize for."

Still, the guilt weighed on him. The best thing he could do was put some distance between them before he did something else to mess things up even further. He didn't want her to leave. He told himself that he wanted her to stay because she didn't have anywhere else to go, but was that the only reason?

"I should get back to the field." He turned and headed for the door.

He could feel Cherie's gaze on his back as he made his hasty departure, but he refused to turn back. There was something about her—something that got to him in a way no one else ever had. And for a man who prided himself on not being afraid of anything, the tsunami of emotions she stirred up in him scared him.

CHAPTER SEVEN

SHE'D NEVER BEEN kissed so passionately before.

At least she didn't think so.

Cherie's fingers traced her tingling lips as she clearly recalled the heat in their kiss. So she hadn't been mistaken when she thought he'd been considering kissing her yesterday in the driveway.

And it had been so much better than her imagination had conjured up. Her whole body had come to life in his arms. She'd forgotten about where they were or how they'd met just a few days ago.

It felt as if they'd known each other for a long time. The way he'd confided in her was like they were old friends. She loved that he felt so comfortable around her that she opened up about his past. She would share some of hers, but she still didn't have a clue who she was or where she belonged. What would happen when she did remember her past? Would this thing between them continue to grow?

She recalled how he'd pulled away from her after the kiss. It had been so abrupt. And then she remembered how he'd insisted on apologizing to her. She wasn't so sure there would be a second kiss. Though she couldn't help but hope she was wrong.

But would the attraction linger after her memory returned? She didn't know the answer, but she couldn't imagine not having her heart pitter-patter in his presence.

She continued to search for the cleaning supplies. When she came across a back hallway, she found everything she was looking for. There was an old vacuum. Stacks of dusting rags. There were even cleaning products. Not nearly enough to clean this whole place, but it was enough to get her started.

She set to work in the kitchen. She began working in one corner and then proceeded to make her way around in a counterclockwise fashion. She cleaned the floor, followed by the cabinets and then the wall. By the time she finished, she realized that she had to redo her work as the heavy dust from the upper cabinets had fallen onto the counters and the floor that she'd previously cleaned.

The truth was she had no idea what she was

doing. If she was going to be a housekeeper at the hotel, why didn't she have the instincts of someone who worked in that profession?

Her painted pink nails were now chipped. Why were her nails so long if she spent her time cleaning this or that? It didn't seem very practical. But then again, she could have been on holiday. She closed her eyes and focused hard on her past, hoping for just a glimmer of a memory. After all, the doctor said her memory may come back little by little or all at once, but so far she had no glimpses of her past. What would she do if it never came back?

The question weighed on her. She couldn't imagine never remembering who she was, or her family. She had to believe her memory would return. Hopefully, sooner rather than later.

She threw the rag into the pail of bleach water that she'd been using to clean the window. The water splashed up, landing on her shorts. She tried to wipe it off but it was too late. The wet droplets turned the blue of her shorts to white spots. She groaned. She couldn't continue to ruin her clothes.

In her search to find the cleaning supplies, she recalled finding some housekeeper outfits in the little bedroom off the kitchen. She rushed there to find the gray-and-white uniforms hanging in the closet.

As she held one up to herself, she found it to be too large. They'd need to be altered. She searched the room, looking for a needle and thread. When she found a sewing basket, she picked it up.

Suddenly she had a flashback of another sewing box. It was a silver box. It had brightly colored threads and a small red pillow holding dozens of pins.

As quickly as the memory came to her, it was gone. A smile pulled at her lips. She'd remembered something. This had to be the beginning of more memories.

She closed her eyes, trying to retrieve more of her past. She focused on the image of the sewing box. Where had she seen it? Was she a seamstress in addition to being a housekeeper? The answers refused to come to her.

Maybe this evening, when she was in the cottage altering the uniforms, more memories would come to her. She could only hope so.

The next day Antoine stayed in the field until the sun started to sink below the horizon. He told himself that he was working late because he was anxious to get as much work done before he put the place up for sale, but that wasn't the only reason.

He couldn't get the kiss out of his mind. Cherie's face was there in the center of his thoughts. When he was doing manual labor in the field, the thought of her was foremost in his mind. When he closed his eyes at night, he could feel her lips pressed to his. And when he woke in the morning, she was his first thought.

It was crazy. He barely even knew her and yet he was drawn to her. The only thing he knew to do was to avoid her. After all, they both had a job to do. She didn't need him lurking over her shoulder. And so he'd stayed away from the château after the kiss.

Now with the last rays of sunshine in the sky, he headed toward the château. He climbed the steps and entered the front door. He didn't know what he expected when he entered the house, but it wasn't to find the warm glow of a lamp in the foyer. It was as though Cherie had turned it on in anticipation of his return.

It reminded him of when he was a boy and his grandmother would wait for him to get home from a friend's house. She would greet him with a warm smile and ask if he had a good time. While she fed him a late dinner or snack, she would ask about his day. She would sit there sipping tea and listen to him as though it was the most important thing in the world.

In that moment, a pang of sorrow hit him. He'd missed his grandmother's final years on this earth. He'd let his anger with his grandfather drive him away and he'd stood on his stubborn pride, refusing to return. In the end, when he had returned it was for his grandmother's funeral.

By then it was too late to tell her how sorry he was for being absent from her life—how he'd let his anger toward his grandfather overshadow his love for her. And now both of his grandparents were gone, as was his mother. And he was left with this mausoleum of memories.

As determined as he was to sell the château and leave the past behind him, he still hadn't brought himself to make the call to the real-estate agent. He told himself that he was just waiting until he got some more work done around the place so he could request a proper amount for the estate. It had nothing to do with his difficulty of letting go of the only place that had ever been a real home to him.

Cherie stepped into the foyer. "I thought I heard someone."

He was surprised to see her at this late hour. "It's just me. I didn't expect to see you."

A brief frown crossed her face, but she subdued it. "I was working late. I started dinner for you."

He wondered what she'd cooked. "What is it?"

"Nothing fancy," she said. "If I can cook, I can't remember. But I found some old cookbooks to guide me."

He sniffed the air. Instead of a delicious aroma, it smelled like something was burning. "When was the last time you checked on dinner?"

At that point, she smelled the foul scent, too. "Oh, no!"

She ran back to the kitchen. He was hot on her heels. She opened the oven and the smoke rolled into the kitchen.

"It's ruined." Her voice sounded so dejected.

"Maybe it's salvageable." He turned to open the windows and realized they were all clean. She'd been working hard.

Cherie took the pot over to the sink and turned on the water. "Not unless you like your food well-charred."

Definitely not. He watched as her shoulders slumped. He felt bad for her and wanted to cheer her up. "At least you know that cooking isn't one of your talents."

"Neither is cleaning."

"Why would you say that? The kitchen looks really good, and the foyer is getting there."

"In the process I splashed bleach on my clothes and ruined them. That's why I'm wearing this." She turned to him.

In the bright light of the kitchen, he was able to take in her maid's uniform. He swallowed hard. The uniform had never looked so good.

The V-neck gave just a hint of her rounded cleavage. The shirt was gathered at the waist by the matching skirt. A white apron pulled it all together. The skirt was short, much too short for a traditional look. It stopped a few centimeters above her knees, giving him a good view of her legs. He swallowed hard.

How was he supposed to avoid thinking about kissing her when she looked so good? So very good. He longed to pull her into his arms. He grasped the table next to him to keep himself from going to her.

Cherie fingered the lace edge of the apron. "I know I should have asked before taking it."

"No. It's fine." Very fine indeed.

"I had to make some modifications because it didn't fit me."

He swallowed. "It definitely fits you now."

Color rose in her cheeks. "I—I should clean up this mess."

If he didn't get out of there immediately, he knew he would make his way over to her and press his lips to the curve of her neck. And that would just be the beginning of things.

"I'll run out and get us some food. I'll be back." He didn't wait for her to respond as he turned and retraced his steps to the front door.

He could only hope she would change into something else before he returned. He wasn't sure he would make it through dinner with her in that little housekeeper outfit.

He already knew the image that would dance through his dreams tonight. The image of her in that uniform was tattooed on his mind. He was in so much trouble.

She'd made a mess of dinner.

And yet Antoine hadn't minded.

Cherie sat across from him at the kitchen table. Their plates were now empty, and she knew she should clean up and head back to the cottage, but she couldn't draw herself away from him.

He'd changed before dinner from his dirty

work clothes into something more casual. He now wore dark jeans and a collared shirt with the sleeves rolled up. He looked incredibly handsome.

She felt self-conscious in her uniform. She should have gone to the cottage to change clothes before they ate, but she'd been in such a rush to clean the kitchen that she hadn't had a chance to change.

As much as she didn't want this evening to end, the food was eaten and the conversation had dwindled to nothing. It was with the greatest regret that she got to her feet. "I should clean this up before going."

He stood, too. "Let me help you."

They both reached for the same empty food container. Immediately her fingertips tingled. A current of awareness pulsated up her arm and set her heart pitter-pattering. When she turned her head, their gazes met and held.

Oh, my!

There was heat in the depths of his dark eyes. He desired her. Her stomach dipped. She longed for him, too.

"I've got it." Antoine lifted the container from her grasp, breaking the spell that had come over her. With his plate in the other hand, he turned toward the kitchen.

It took her a moment to gather her wits

about her. She took the other food container and plate. She followed him into the kitchen. She shouldn't just drop the dirty dishes in the sink and leave them for later.

Instead she added dish soap to the hot water. Soap suds filled the sink. She plunged her hands into the soapy water.

"You don't have to do this." His deep voice sent a shiver of excitement up her spine.

"I want to."

He stepped closer. Her heart rate sped up. She told herself that his close proximity meant nothing, but she wasn't that good of a liar. He reached past her to place a glass in the sink. After he released the glass into the soapy water, his fingers touched hers. The breath caught in her throat. Did he know how hard he was making it for her to act indifferent?

As his fingertips moved over hers, her rational thoughts started to short-circuit. All she could think about was how good his touch felt and how she longed to feel more of it.

Apparently, she'd failed to keep her desire under wraps. Antoine's front pressed against her back. Her heart pounded wildly. She fought the urge to lean back into him.

His other hand slid down her arm and plunged into the suds. His fingers threaded through hers.

When he spoke, his breath brushed over the sensitive part of her neck, sending goose bumps cascading down her arms. "I'm suddenly desiring a bubble bath."

Her thoughts meandered to the image of them in one of the large clawfoot tubs upstairs. But to do that would mean moving and she had no desire to move from her place in his arms.

When his lips pressed to the curve of her neck, she gasped. Her entire body was thrumming with need. He trailed a line of kisses up her neck. The fight left her as she leaned back against him.

Aching to feel his lips on hers, she turned to him. Her soft curves pressed against his hard planes. Oh, my, it was getting so hot in the kitchen.

Their gazes met before his attention lowered to her mouth. She wasn't going to wait for him to make his move. She lifted up on her tiptoes and leaned forward, claiming his lips with her own.

He didn't move at first. It was though she'd stunned him with her forwardness. But something told her she wasn't the shy type. When she knew what she wanted, she went after it. And right now, she wanted every single scrumptious centimeter of Antoine.

CHAPTER EIGHT

HE AWOKE EARLY the next morning.

And he wasn't alone.

Antoine didn't move at first. He didn't want to wake Cherie. They'd been up most of the night and she seemed so relaxed now.

His thoughts rolled back in time. Last night, he'd been unbearably tempted beyond all hope of resistance. There was something special about Cherie. She had worked her way past his well-laid defenses and left him longing for more of her.

He'd tried to talk to her before things had gone so far. He'd started to say it might not be a good idea for them to make love, but she'd shushed him. She'd pressed her rosy lips to his once more—her tongue had slipped past his lips and her fingers had crept up the back of his neck to comb through his hair—and his will had snapped. His pounding heart had echoed in his ears, drowning out his thoughts.

His desires had taken over. He had met her kiss for kiss. It had been the most amazing night of his life.

And now he watched as she slept so peacefully. It was as if she didn't have a care in the world. He knew that wasn't the case, but for now he let her have her happy dreams.

He enjoyed the feel of her snuggled up to him. In fact, he liked it too much. He could see himself getting used to this arrangement. And that couldn't happen.

He knew it was only a matter of time until Cherie remembered who she really was and then she'd be gone. That's how it should be. He didn't want to hold her back from her life.

Cherie was like a force of nature. She'd turned his life upside down and she was starting to make the château into a home again. Day by day. Room by room.

Even though last night had been amazing, he knew he couldn't let it happen again. He couldn't let either of them think this thing between them was based on reality, especially when neither of them knew her real identity. The best thing he could do for both of them was forget it ever happened—like that was possible.

And lying here was not helping matters. He had to move. He had to get out in the field.

He glanced over at the clock on the bedside stand. He was late.

Ever so gently, he freed himself from Cherie. When she lightly moaned and rolled over, he froze. He waited until her breathing returned to its even rhythm. Then he got out of bed, careful to avoid the squeaky floorboards—something he'd learned to do as a kid.

A quick shower later, he dressed in jeans and a T-shirt. He didn't bother to shave. He hadn't touched a razor in days. A layer of stubble lined his jaw. He was starting to get used to it.

With one last glance at Cherie, he turned and headed for the door. He paused in the kitchen to grab something to eat, but then he glanced at the sink, still filled with now-cold water and dishes. He didn't want her to wake up to a mess in the kitchen.

He started some coffee. Even though he was late to meet up with his men, he stayed and cleaned the dishes. Once they were put away, his appetite was long forgotten. He quickly downed a cup of coffee. He thought of leaving Cherie a note, but he had no idea what to say to her. *Hey, last night was great but we can't do it again* or *you're amazing but I'm not the man for you*. He couldn't bring himself to write any of those things. Instead, he quietly headed out the door. They'd talk later. Much later.

Things had changed.

And in some ways, they'd stayed the same.

Cherie sat up in bed, clutching the sheet to her chest as she glanced around the large room. Dust covers were draped over most of the furniture. On the end of the bed, her clothes were neatly folded, but Antoine was nowhere to be seen.

She fell back against the soft pillows. She stretched out like a purring cat lounging in the afternoon sun. Her mind replayed the events of the prior evening. A smile tugged at the corners of her lips.

Antoine had been a passionate lover. Her body tingled with the memory. It had been the most amazing night.

In the next breath, she knew there couldn't be a repeat. She didn't know who she was or what her life was like before her accident. She was in absolutely no position to start a relationship. It wouldn't be fair to either one of them.

She recalled how Antoine had tried to slow things down before they'd spun deliciously out of control. She winced at the memory of how she'd smothered his words of reason with her hungry kisses. Now, in the light of day, she realized he was right. It shouldn't have happened.

He might not want a repeat of their night together, but if he did, she would need to let him down gently. She couldn't explain what had gotten into her last night, but she wouldn't lose control again.

And yet every time she thought of Antoine and how she felt wrapped in his muscled arms, her heart raced. She tamped down her reaction to the thought of him. It wouldn't help the situation.

When she checked the time, she was shocked to find it was midway through the morning. She'd best get to it. She didn't want Antoine to think she expected their arrangement to change because they'd slept together.

So far, she'd learned that she wasn't good in the kitchen… Scratch that—she was a disaster in the kitchen. She wasn't afraid to be forward when there was something she was passionate about. And now, she knew she liked to keep her word.

With that in mind, she scrambled out of bed and dressed. On her way to the guesthouse, she was surprised to find the kitchen had been tidied up. She was quite certain they'd left the dinner dishes in the sink, so that meant Antoine had taken time to clean them that morning. She smiled. It was thoughtful of him.

After showering and putting on a fresh uniform, she decided to finish cleaning the foyer. Considering it wasn't a small room, it took her a lot of time. She couldn't believe the amount of antiques she'd found in that room alone. It made her nervous each time she picked up a statue.

She just had to dust this one large vase on the stand by the door and she would be done with this room. She was thinking of cleaning Antoine's room next. She felt bad that he'd given up the cottage in order to let her stay there. She wanted his room to be comfortable for him after a long day in the fields.

She picked up the vase just as the front door swung open behind her. Before she could move out of the way, the door bumped into her. She lurched forward. In her attempt not to lose her balance, she lost her grasp on the vase.

Her hip collided with the edge of the small table. The vase flew through the air. It crashed to the floor. Cherie stared at the heap of broken porcelain in horror.

No. No. No. This can't have happened.

"Cherie?" Antoine appeared from behind

the door. When he saw her bent over the table, he rushed to her side. He reached out to her, placing his hand on her upper arm. "Are you alright?"

She straightened. Her skin tingled beneath the touch of his fingers. "I'm fine, but that beautiful vase isn't. I'm so sorry. I was trying to be so careful."

He stared into her eyes for a moment longer than was necessary. Her heart beat faster. Was he having thoughts of picking up where they'd left off last night?

No. That can't happen. It is best to pretend it never happened.

He lowered his hand to his side, leaving behind a cold spot on her arm where his touch had just been. His gaze moved to the broken porcelain scattered over the floor. "It's not your fault."

"Yes, it is. I dropped it. I should have been holding on to it better."

"Or perhaps I shouldn't have come flying through the door and bumped into you."

She wanted to argue with him, but she couldn't. "Perhaps it's both of our faults. I'd offer to replace it but I'm guessing it's very old and irreplaceable."

"It's okay. If you haven't noticed, this place is filled with antiques."

"It definitely is. It's going to take me forever to dust all of the display cases and their contents."

"Don't worry about those details for now. Just focus on cleaning the rest of the rooms."

"I will."

"I just stopped to grab some money. I need to run into the village for some supplies. Do you need anything?"

"I do need a few things."

"Good. We'll go together. I'll be right back." He bounded up the stairs.

She bent over to start cleaning up the broken vase. All the while she wondered if she should change out of her uniform. She wasn't so sure Antoine wanted to be seen in public with his housekeeper.

True to his word, Antoine quickly returned. She straightened. She would finish cleaning up the mess when they got back. She didn't want to hold up Antoine since he was so nice to offer her a ride.

When he reached the bottom of the stairs, he stopped next to her. "I have an idea." He tossed her the keys. "You drive."

Drive? His fancy little sports car?

She wasn't so comfortable with that proposition. She wasn't even sure she could drive. But everyone knew how to drive, didn't they?

She hated this amnesia. She didn't know what she'd forgotten and what she truly didn't know. And she hated the helpless sensation it elicited in her.

"What's wrong?"

"Um…nothing." She didn't want to admit the truth.

"It's definitely something. I can see the worry lines on your face. So out with it."

"I'm not comfortable driving your car."

"You mean because it's a manual transmission."

She hadn't thought of that. She searched her memory for some inkling of knowledge about driving and drew a blank.

"Don't worry about it," he said. "I could get one of the trucks from the vineyard."

She shook her head. "You aren't understanding. I'm not sure I can drive any vehicle."

"Oh." To his credit, he kept the surprise from his face.

"But who doesn't know how to drive?" She was frustrated with herself. She lowered her gaze to the floor. How was she supposed to be independent when she couldn't do some of the basic things?

He approached her. "Maybe you do know how and you just can't remember."

"Maybe." But she had her doubts.

He placed a finger beneath her chin and raised it until their gazes met. "Is this really that important to you?"

She shrugged instead of admitting that it was very important to her.

He withdrew his hand, though they were still connected via their gazes. "Then I'll give you a driving lesson."

"You will?" She couldn't believe he was willing to take the time out of his day to help her. And then she felt guilty because he had other priorities. "I couldn't ask you to do that."

"You aren't. I'm volunteering."

She couldn't wait to try driving. Excitement flooded her veins. She was so anxious to find out what she was capable of and equally horrified at the possibility of wrecking his sports car.

He should have said something.

Antoine sat quietly in the passenger seat of one of the vineyard trucks with an automatic transmission while Cherie worked the controls. He thought it might be easier for her than his car. He'd intended their driving lesson to be curtailed to the long driveway, but she had excelled to the point where she was navigating them into the village.

She didn't need his help. She knew exactly what she was doing behind the steering wheel. Stretching her wings had been good for her. He caught the glint of confidence in her eyes as she'd negotiated her way through a busy intersection.

Since he'd gotten up that morning, he'd been gearing himself to tell Cherie that they couldn't continue sleeping together. It just made things too messy. What would happen when she got her memory back and left? Or what would happen when the time came for him to return to Paris? Would she want to go with him? Would he want her to?

Besides, he didn't have the time to devote to a relationship. He had the estate and his business that needed his undivided attention. He was a workaholic, according to his assistant. The term didn't bother him, probably because it was accurate. He always had to be busy.

But the truth was that everyone he'd loved, he had lost. He couldn't bear to lose someone else that he cared for. And when Cherie's memories came back to her, she would return to her former life. And that would be it for their relationship.

He glanced over at her, wondering if she even wanted another night with him. He noticed how her demeanor was different than last night—quieter and more reserved. Did that mean he was the only one who'd enjoyed their night together? Images of their lovemaking flashed in his mind. No, that definitely wasn't the case.

"It's coming back to me." Her voice cut through his thoughts.

"That's great. Anything else coming back to you?"

Internally, he struggled between wanting her to have her memory back and wanting her to stay at the château a bit longer. He knew it was selfish to want her to stick around, but there was something about having her around that had him looking forward to the evenings, when he knew he would see her.

"Not really. Only that I know how to sew."

"It's a start. The rest will follow."

"I hope so."

He knew she was anxious to get back to her life. He couldn't confuse things for her. Because in the end, he wasn't the man for her. He couldn't offer her things like marriage, children and forever.

He'd been through enough trauma as a kid with his mother's death and his father missing from his life. To this day, he didn't even know his father's name. Who didn't know their father's name?

According to his grandparents, they didn't know who his father was. It was a secret that his mother took to her grave. The unknown identity of the man had nagged at him throughout his life.

There were questions he had about his father—questions about himself. Was he anything like his father? Why had he walked away? Did his father even know about him?

The thoughts gnawed at him as they shopped in the village. All of this stuff about Cherie not remembering her past reminded him of the holes in his own life. Unlike Cherie, he'd come to the realization that he was never going to find the answer about his paternity. And it wasn't from the lack of trying. He'd scoured the internet and hired a private investigator. There simply weren't enough clues to go on.

Cherie picked up some cleaning products and a new vacuum. He bought some supplies to use in the fields. And finally they walked through the market, choosing their meals together.

It wasn't until they were back at the château that he worked up the nerve to have this awkward conversation with her. He didn't want to hurt her. That was the very last thing he wanted to do. And by ending the romantic part of their relationship now, he hoped it would hurt her less than if they let this thing between them continue and then it had to end later.

They'd just finished putting the food away and he checked the time. Half of the afternoon was already gone. He needed to take the supplies to his men. But first, they had to have this conversation.

"Cherie, can we talk?"

She turned to him. "I thought that's what we've been doing."

"It is, but there's something else we need to discuss." He struggled to find the right words. "It's about last night."

He stepped toward her and then realized it was probably a mistake, because if he was close enough to touch her…the difficult words he needed to speak would die in his throat and instead, he'd pull her into his arms and press a kiss to her pouty lips.

"What about it?" Her gaze searched his.

"I think we need to take a step back." He stopped there, waiting for her reaction.

"You don't want to continue what we started?"

His body tensed as he struggled not to follow his desires and to do the right thing. "I think it was late and we were both tired and perhaps not thinking clearly."

It was a flimsy excuse. He knew exactly what he was doing last night and he longed to do it again. But the price was too high for both of them.

When it came time for Cherie to return to her life, she didn't need to be weighed down with complications. She'd already gone through so much with her memory loss.

Cherie didn't say anything.

He rested his hands on his waist. "It was great and everything, but it can't continue."

If she was surprised, or hurt, she didn't let it show on her face. "I understand."

That was it. Two words uttered, devoid of emotion. He kept waiting for something more—her anger, or her disappointment. Instead, he got nothing but a stoic expression.

He wasn't going to push things. He'd said what he needed to. It was best he returned to work. And so with a quick goodbye, he was out the door. All the while, he kept wondering if they'd be able to rewind time and act like that night of passion hadn't happened.

CHAPTER NINE

HE'D REJECTED HER.

No one had ever rejected her.

Cherie didn't know how she knew that, but something told her she wasn't used to rejection. Maybe that's why his words still stung more than a few days later.

Sure, she was going to tell him much the same thing, but she hadn't expected him to say it first—for him not to want her again. She'd thought he'd enjoyed their night as much as she had. Apparently that hadn't been the case. The acknowledgment dug at a tender spot in her chest.

And now things between them were awkward.

It was the only word to explain their current relationship.

They'd barely spoken to each other since that conversation. She kept herself busy cleaning as quickly as she could. He spent most of his waking hours in the vineyard.

She ate all of her meals in the guesthouse... alone. He took his meals in the solitude of the main house. It was all very uncomfortable.

She just needed to complete her job and move on. But cleaning a château of this size was not a quick or easy task. In the week she had been working on it, she had only cleaned the kitchen, foyer and Antoine's bedroom. Who lived in places this big?

She rolled the vacuum along behind her as she moved to the den at the back of the house. She swung open the large door and was greeted by long shadows. Like every other room in the château, the heavy drapes were drawn.

She started there. With a ladder, she removed the drapes from a long rod. The material was old and sun-faded, but Antoine had made no mention of replacing any of the items. And so she laid the drapes in the growing stack in the laundry room. She would have to speak with Antoine about whether he wanted to send them out to be cleaned, which is what she thought should be done, or if he wanted her to try putting them in the old washing machine. She didn't think they'd fair too well that way.

Now that the sunlight had been allowed in, she gazed around the room. She tried to decide where to start. One wall was lined with bookcases. The wood was a rich, dark shade. The shelves were lined with books.

In that moment, she had a flashback to another set of bookshelves, but before she was able to grasp on to the memory, it disintegrated and left her longing to recapture it. Try as she might, the memory was gone. She was left to wonder what it was she'd remembered.

With a resigned sigh, she let go of the faded memory and moved toward the enormous desk. It dominated the room. It appeared Antoine had been using it for his work in the evening.

Perhaps she would clean off the desk and then start with the walls. She grabbed her duster and moved to the desk. She pulled out the chair. It would need some polish, but it could wait until she'd cleaned up the desk.

As she stared at the top of the desk, she was careful to keep everything in its place. When she lifted the desk pad to dust under it, she noticed a white envelope. She wouldn't have given it a second glance if it hadn't been for the name on the envelope. Scrawled over the front of the envelope in black ink was Antoine's name and address. There was even a stamp on it, as though whoever had written it was planning on mailing it, but had never gotten the chance.

She should just leave it, but something in her drove her to pick it up. The envelope was sealed, which told her that Antoine had yet to read its contents. Perhaps it was important. Maybe whatever was inside would affect the sale of the estate.

With that thought in mind, she shoved the envelope in her pocket. She would give it to Antoine before she left for the evening.

While she was vacuuming the floor, there was a tap on her shoulder. She jumped. With a hand pressed to her chest, she turned. Antoine was standing there.

She rushed to turn off the vacuum. "Is something wrong?"

He shook his head. "It's late."

She glanced back at the window to see that the sun had set. She'd gotten so caught up in her work that she hadn't even noticed. "I just wanted to finish this room."

"It can be finished tomorrow." His gaze met hers. "Did you even stop to eat dinner?"

She shook her head as her stomach rumbled. She was certain he wanted her gone so he could work on his emails in silence. "I'll just put these things away and get out of your way."

"You could join me for a late dinner, if you want."

She wanted to, but she wasn't sure if she should accept the invitation. Perhaps he was just being polite. That was probably it, because this was the most he'd spoken to her all week.

"I don't want to disturb you." She moved to unplug the vacuum. "I'll just go back to the guesthouse."

"You won't be disturbing me. I'm sorry things have gotten to the point where you aren't comfortable sharing a meal with me. I'd like to find a way to fix things. Do you think that's possible?"

She didn't trust herself to speak. She didn't want to appear too eager. Instead, she nodded. She would like nothing more because she'd been so lonely without his presence this week.

He had missed her.

He didn't want the evening to end.

Antoine stacked the dishes next to the sink. They were not going to attempt to wash them. He remembered what had happened the last time they'd washed dishes together. He recalled the moment with crystal clarity.

"I can wash those for you," Cherie said.

"That's okay. They can wait until tomorrow." He glanced around at the cabinets. "I think I'm going to have a dishwasher installed."

"It sounds like you're starting to settle into the place."

"That, or I really don't like washing dishes." Which wasn't exactly the truth, because if they did the dishes the same way they had last time, he'd never want a dishwasher ever again.

"You'll be pleased to know that I'm almost done cleaning the den."

"I appreciate you making the rooms I use a priority."

A smile bloomed on her face. "I'm just trying to help."

He loved how her smile reached up and touched her eyes. "If you need help with any of it, just let me know."

"I will." She glanced away. "There is one thing."

"What's that?" He hoped it was something where they could spend more time together.

"It's the drapes. They were filthy so I took them down. I have stacked them in the laundry room. I could try putting them in the washing machine but I'm not sure in their condition that they'll survive."

"So what you're saying is that I need to purchase new ones?"

"Uh, yes."

"I'll put my assistant on it."

"Your assistant?" She looked puzzled.

"Yes, she's a master of all things. Don't worry. I pay her well for all of the extras she does for me."

"Oh. I wasn't thinking that. I was just wondering if you'd want to pick out the drapes yourself."

He shook his head. "Since I'm not keeping this place, I don't care about those details. As long as they look nice for the potential buyers, I'll be good with them."

"Okay. I'll make sure I move the drapes outside to have them hauled away."

"Just leave them where they are. I'll have them removed."

"Thanks. I should be going. I'm sure you have things to do before you call it a night." She started for the door before she turned back to him. "I'm running out of some cleaning supplies. I was wondering if I could borrow the truck to drive into the village."

"Sure. You've already proven that you have a lot of experience driving. And here…" He reached in his pocket and withdrew some money. "Take this."

She waved it off. "I still have money from what you paid me."

He looked horrified. "That money isn't for you to spend on things for the estate. It's for you to do with what you want. You earned it."

She looked hesitant, but then she accepted the additional money. When she went to put it in her pocket, her eyes widened. She withdrew an envelope. "I totally forgot about this."

"What is it?"

"I don't know. I found it in the office." She held it out to him, but when he didn't go to take it from her, she said, "It has your name on it."

His gaze moved from her to the envelope. He recognized the handwriting. It was his grandfather's. "I don't want to read it."

"But it might be something important."

He briefly glanced at the envelope again. "I doubt it."

"How can you be sure?"

"Because that's my grandfather's handwriting. And anything he would have to say to me wouldn't be worth the effort of reading." When her eyebrows rose and surprise reflected in her eyes, he knew how horrible he must have sounded. "My grandfather and I had a contentious relationship. Nothing I ever did was good enough."

This wasn't a conversation he planned on having while standing by the door. He thought of moving to the living room, where it was more comfortable, but it might be too comfy, especially with Cherie so close by.

Instead, he pulled out a kitchen chair. "Why don't you sit down?"

Still holding the envelope, she moved and took a seat. "You don't have to talk about this if you don't want to."

He never talked about his past. It wasn't that it was a big dark secret. It was more that he didn't want to revisit the unsettling time in his life.

Still, this was his chance to explain why he wasn't keeping the estate so Cherie would stop trying to change his mind. It wasn't going to happen. His future was in Paris, not Saint-Tropez.

"Growing up, my grandfather had been a big, strong man. He worked all day doing manual labor. He didn't believe in being lazy. And so he rarely took a day off. He drove himself and those around him to work hard."

"So that's where you get your work ethic."

Antoine shrugged. He'd never thought of it before, but he supposed she was right. "I guess so. But it didn't matter how hard I worked, it was never good enough for him."

She reached out and covered his hand with her own. She gave it a squeeze. No words were spoken. Just the simple gesture was enough for him to feel her support. It propelled him onward with his story.

Antoine cleared his throat. "My grandfather never said it, but I know he blamed me for my mother's death. According to my grandmother, my mother had been the light of his life. And if I hadn't been born, she would still be alive."

She gasped. "Did he say that to you?"

"No. But it was there every day with his frowns and curt words."

Her hand continued to rest on his. "I'm sorry."

He sighed. "It wasn't all my grandfather. It was the kids in school. You know how tough they can be. Because I didn't have a mother and I didn't know who my father was, I would make up stories about my father. I would pretend he was an explorer, climbing Mount Everest and hiking through the Amazon. But when he never showed up at any of my school programs, the kids stopped believing me. And then the merciless teasing began."

"How horrible. It must have been so hard for you."

He'd never spoken of the bullying he'd endured in school, not even with his grandmother. So why did he mention it now? It was over and done with. No one teased him now. These days he was a self-made man who commanded respect with his business prowess.

"It's all in the past." He'd hoped to close the door on the subject.

"Maybe you could use your experience to help your children when you have them."

He shook his head. "There won't be any kids."

"You sound very certain."

"I am." He'd never had a father in his life, not even for one solitary day, so how was he supposed to know anything about fatherhood?

"What if your wife wants a child?"

"It's doubtful that I'll get married, but if I were to, I would tell her upfront about my unwillingness to have children. She will understand that the subject is nonnegotiable." Not wanting to discuss himself any longer, he turned the table on her. "And what about you? Will you one day have children?"

She paused as though searching for the answer. "I don't know. I still can't remember anything about my past."

"What about the new you? Does the idea of

children appeal to you?" He hoped she'd say she didn't want kids. As soon as he realized the direction of his thoughts, he halted them.

"Actually, I do think I'd like at least one baby." A dreamy smile came over her face, as though she was imagining holding an infant in her arms. "But, of course, I'd have to meet the right man first."

An awkward silence fell over them. He couldn't help but wonder if she had someone special waiting for her. The faraway look on her face had him assuming she was having a similar thought.

"I believe you'll get your memory back and have the life you want, including a baby." He just wouldn't be a part of that future. The acknowledgement weighed on him.

Her gaze moved to the envelope. "Aren't you curious about what your grandfather had to say?"

"Would it be wrong if I said no?"

She shook her head. "What was your grandmother like?"

"She was kind and loving. She wanted to see the good in everyone. And she missed my mother dearly. She kept my mother's bedroom exactly as she'd left it." He delved back into the memories that he hadn't thought of in many years. "I remember the door was always closed. Once in a while I would sneak in there, but not often because it was sad in there. All of her things were left exactly as she had put them, as though my grandparents were just waiting for her to return home."

"I can't even imagine what that must have been like."

His gaze lifted to meet hers. Here she was feeling sorry for him and she couldn't even remember her own family. "I shouldn't be telling you all of this. You have enough on your mind."

"It's nice to focus on someone else for a change. It sounds like your grandparents loved and missed your mother dearly."

"They did. I think her death changed both of them greatly." The memories came rushing back to him. "I remember one time as a small boy I was supposed to be asleep, but I got hungry. I was just returning from the kitchen when I saw my grandfather coming out of my mother's room. I hid so he wouldn't see me. I didn't want to get in trouble for being up past my bedtime. I remember seeing the tears in his eyes. It was something I'll never forget because my grandfather wasn't an emotional person. The only other time I saw him cry was at my grandmother's funeral."

"It sounds like he struggled after your mother died."

He nodded. "I can see that now. But back then I just didn't think he loved me. I couldn't wait to move away. I was about to finish at the university, which I attended at my grandmother's insistence. She believed in education and she wanted the world for me. Anyway, when I came home that last time, there was a big blowup with my grandfather. He said now that I was finished with school that it was time for me to do some real work."

"He wanted you to help him run the vineyard?"

Antoine shook his head. "I don't think my grandfather wanted anyone but him running the vineyard. He was a bit of a control freak. But he wanted me there to do the manual labor—to be at his beck and call. He said that's what all good grandsons would do."

Her gaze returned to the envelope. "Maybe he regretted his actions."

"Doubtful." Still, her words had him curious to know what his grandfather had to say.

He grasped the envelope. He noticed that it had been addressed and stamped. It was though his grandfather had written it just before he passed away in his sleep—before he'd had a chance to mail it.

Perhaps it was time. Antoine loosened the flap on the envelope and pulled out the folded page. His chest tightened as he waited to find out what his grandfather's last words were to him.

Antoine,
I'm writing to you to beg your forgiveness. I know I wasn't the grandfather you wanted or deserved.

Your grandmother tried to tell me I was being too hard on you, but I couldn't hear her. I only ever wanted the best for you.

Now, with your grandmother gone, I'm all alone in this big old house with my regrets. I'm surrounded by the voices from the past.

I'm sorry. I only ever wanted to protect you. Something I failed to do for your mother. I never did learn the name of your father. I tried my best, but times were different then and there weren't computers to track everything.

In the end, I drove you away. That was not something I wanted. I always thought that someday it would be you and I who worked this land together.

I know you're busy, but I was hop-

*ing you would consider coming home to
visit.*

We could start over.

I will always be here for you.

I love you,

Papi

A tear splashed onto the page. Antoine
swiped at his eyes. He couldn't believe his
grandfather had written this letter and yet it
was most definitely his grandfather's distinc-
tive handwriting.

"Antoine?" Cherie's voice held a note of
concern.

He held the letter out for her. He sat quietly
while she read the heartfelt words his grandfather had written. If his grandfather had
lived long enough to mail the letter, would
Antoine have gone to meet with him?

He would never know the answer to that
question. He'd like to think he would have
gotten past his pride and gone to his grandfather. He liked to think they would have
formed a new relationship—one that was
much warmer.

Now that moment was lost to him. And so
was any chance of finding his father. He was
shocked to read that his grandfather had no

idea who his father was. If Papi didn't know, the truth was, in fact, lost to him.

Cherie handed the letter back to him. "How does that make you feel?"

"Like we wasted a lot of years."

"So if he were here today instead of me, would you have forgiven him?"

Antoine paused to give the idea some thought. So many conditions would go into that answer that he really didn't know. "I guess we'll never know."

"But you're here now. Maybe you and this beautiful estate can have a second chance. Maybe you could reconsider raising a family here and do it different than your grandfather—the way you wished you'd been raised."

"No." He shook his head. "I wouldn't even know how to be a good father."

"You're a compassionate man. Look what you've done for me, and I was a complete stranger. Imagine what you'd be willing to do for someone you loved." She got to her feet. "You have a lot to think about so I should be going. Good night."

And then she walked away, leaving him alone with his thoughts—with his regrets. He hated regrets because there was nothing you could do with them. He couldn't undo the past. He couldn't change what had been done. All he could do is try to learn from it and not repeat those mistakes—the mistakes his grandfather had made while raising him. And the best way not to repeat the past was not to have any children.

CHAPTER TEN

A COUPLE OF days later, Cherie was sitting in Dr. Tournet's office. The morning sunshine shone through the frosted window of the exam room.

She wrung her hands.

She'd already been poked and prodded. Her stitches had been removed. And though her facial bruising hadn't faded much, it was progressing as expected. Her broken nose had been examined and it was determined that it was healing properly. No surgery was required.

Now she was waiting in an exam room for her test results to see if the brain scan showed anything that might explain her continued memory loss. The longer the amnesia persisted, the more stressed she became. What if she never recovered her memories?

Antoine reached out and squeezed her hand. "It's going to be alright."

"What if it's not? I don't know if I can go through the rest of my life without remembering my family. Each night I go to bed hoping when I wake that my memories will have returned. But it never happens."

Knock-knock.

Dr. Tournet opened the door and stepped inside. His expression was blank as he moved to the stool next to a computer. His fingers moved rapidly over the keyboard.

Cherie squeezed Antoine's hand tightly as her anticipation grew. What was taking the doctor so long to reveal the results? She was torn between wanting something to show up to explain her lack of memory and not wanting anything to be wrong.

When she couldn't take the silence any longer, she asked, "Did you find anything?"

Dr. Tournet lifted his reading glasses and rested them atop his head. "Your scan is clear. I can't find any physical reason for your prolonged memory loss."

"Oh." She wasn't sure how to react to that information.

Now that she knew there was nothing they could do for her medically, it was all up to her. Was there a subconscious reason she didn't want to recall her past? Was there something traumatic she wanted to block out? Or was she just overthinking things?

She was lost in her thoughts as they made their way back to Antoine's sports car. Instead of turning north toward the vineyard, he turned south toward the heart of Saint-Tropez. Perhaps he had some supplies to pick up for the château.

The town was buzzing with sunseekers, from locals to some celebrities. A number of the women wore colorful sun hats with wide brims. Others just wore dark sunglasses. They made their way along the sidewalks.

She wondered if she lived here. Did she have a small flat along one of these streets just waiting for her to return to it? She concentrated really hard on the passing sites, hoping one of them would strike a memory. Could she be that lucky?

And then Antoine turned onto a street full of colorful shops. He wheeled into the first available parking spot and then turned to her. "Well, don't just sit there. We have some shopping to do."

"Shopping? For what?"

"A swimsuit, of course."

A swimsuit? They were going swimming? Where? There wasn't a pool at the estate. Although there was plenty of room for one behind the château. Hopefully the next couple that lived there would put one in.

"But I have a bikini—in fact, I have a few of them back at the château."

"Let's not waste time driving home when we can just grab what we need right here."

Before she could pepper Antoine with more questions, he got out of the car. She did the same. Antoine was in a particularly good mood. In fact, he took her hand in his as they set off to go shopping.

They visited a few shops until she found the right swimsuit. The bikini was hot pink with white polka dots. She had no idea why it appealed to her, but it did.

Back in the car, she turned to him. "Now where are we going?"

"Did anyone ever tell you that you ask a lot of questions?"

She opened her mouth to answer but then paused. "You know, I have no idea."

She laughed. And then he did, too.

Their destination wasn't far from where they'd gone shopping. They arrived at a members-only beach. Considering it was during the week, the place wasn't overly busy.

They went to the changing rooms. Cherie put on the pink bikini and stared in the mirror. Suddenly the swimsuit seemed so small.

Why hadn't she picked out something a little more modest?

And then she recalled picking out a cover-up. She reached in the bright yellow shopping bag and withdrew the white lace wrap. She slipped it on over her swimsuit. Sure, it was sheer, but it still made her feel better. Was she always self-conscious? She had no idea.

She exited the room to go meet up with Antoine. He was waiting outside for her. When she spotted him, she forgot about her swimsuit because she was too focused on how sexy he looked.

He was lounging against a white stone wall. All he was wearing were a pair of blue board shorts. His broad shoulders were quite tanned, as though he'd been working at the vineyard without a shirt on. She swallowed hard. Maybe she should start walking among the vines and taking in the tantalizing scenery.

His biceps bulged with muscles. And his chest—wow. It was toned, as were his washboard abs. She wished she had a camera because this was an image she never wanted to forget.

He lifted his sunglasses and smiled at her. "See something you like."

Heat flamed in her cheeks as she met

his amused gaze. "You look good." She approached him. "Very good."

"I was thinking the same thing about you."

Things between them had been so much more relaxed ever since she'd found the letter from his grandfather. It was like a wall had come down and now they were once again able to enjoy each other's company.

Just then a young child bumped into her. Cherie fell into Antoine. She put out her hand to help regain her balance and it landed against his muscled chest. It was though an electric current arced between them and raced up her arm, setting her heart racing.

She stared deeply into his eyes. He had the dreamiest eyes. She felt like she could get lost in them.

She should say something, but there was a complete disconnect between her brain and her mouth. It was though time stood still. A part of her knew she should move but her body was rooted in that spot.

It felt like forever since they'd last kissed. The memory of the heated kisses they'd shared taunted her each night in her dreams. Her gaze dipped to his lips.

"We should head down to the beach." Antoine's voice jarred her out of the trance she was in.

She pulled her hand away and stepped back. The heat started in her chest and worked its way up her neck until it settled in her face. "Let's go."

If he was going to pretend that intense moment between them hadn't happened, then she was, too. And so they walked together toward the beach.

"Do you want to go in the water?" he asked.

The sun was hot and seeing Antoine in his swimsuit was making her even more uncomfortable. "I think that's a good idea."

They claimed a table with a big red umbrella. They set aside their towels. And that's when she pulled out the sunscreen she'd picked up in town. She wasn't sure if she burned, but she wasn't taking any chances.

"You can go ahead," she said. "I need to put on some lotion." She held it out to him. "Do you want some?"

He shook his head. "I'm good."

She watched as his eyes widened as she slipped off her cover-up. She struggled not to smile. So he wasn't as immune to her as he liked to pretend. While he watched, she took her time smoothing the lotion over the front of herself. However, she would need some help with her back.

She turned to him and held out the lotion. "Would you mind?"

The muscles in his throat noticeably moved as he swallowed. "Not at all." He took the lotion and squirted some on his hand. "Turn around."

As soon as his fingertips touched the small of her back, she closed her eyes and let herself savor his touch. She longed to turn around and drape her arms around his neck. She imagined her lifting up on her tiptoes to place a kiss on his lips.

And then, all too soon, he finished. "All done. Ready to go?"

With her daydream over, she turned to him. "I am."

Hand in hand, they took off for the water. She had no idea where this day was headed, but she liked it so far. She liked it a whole lot.

Sometimes he had really good ideas.

This was definitely one of them.

He leaned back in a beach chair. He glanced over at Cherie as she ate some fresh fruit. Even with the sunscreen, she'd gotten some sun. She looked beautiful—well, she always looked beautiful, even with her bruises that were finally beginning to fade.

He realized he wanted something to remember this day by. "Do you mind if I run inside?"

"No. Is something wrong?"

"Not at all. I just want to grab my phone. I'll be right back." He stood and headed for the changing rooms. He'd left all of his personal items in a locker.

On his way into the building, he ran into someone he knew. Though he wanted to say a brief hello and keep moving, this was an old friend he hadn't seen in years, so he took a moment to catch up.

By the time he got his phone and headed back to the table, he found his seat was occupied by some man whom he'd never seen before. Antoine paused. What if it was someone who knew Cherie from her other life? Was this what she'd been hoping for? A link to her past?

He wasn't sure what to do. If this was someone who was helping her with her memories, he didn't want to intrude and ruin the moment. Because even if it meant her leaving him, he wanted Cherie to be whole. He wanted her to know her name, her past, her life.

He was about to turn away when he noticed the man reach out and touch Cherie's arm. She jerked it away. The man leaned in closer to her. She leaned back.

Anger stirred in Antoine's gut. How dare that man. Antoine took long, quick steps back to the table. As he neared the table, Cherie stood, as did the man, who reached out to take her hand in his.

"Remove your hand from me." Cherie's voice was stern as she straightened her shoulders. "Now."

The man withdrew his hand. "Come on. We'll have a good time."

"No, we won't." She glowered at him.

The man didn't move and Antoine was out of patience. He stepped in between them. "The lady asked you to leave."

The man pressed his hands to his sides. "Buzz off. The lady and I were having a nice conversation. Weren't we, honey?"

Honey? Was this guy kidding? Antoine wanted to knock some sense into him, but he restrained his temper.

Cherie elbowed Antoine out of the way. She stepped forward. "I'm not your honey and we weren't having a conversation. You need to leave now."

The man glared at her. "You uppity types are all the same."

He stormed off. Antoine had the urge to

follow him and set him straight about Cherie. She was the kindest, most caring person he'd ever known.

And so why was he pushing her away? Maybe she wasn't going to stay forever. Maybe when her memory came back she would leave him for her old life.

But this moment had jarred him into realizing that all they had was this moment. Instead of pushing her away, they could be enjoying themselves.

Cherie turned on him with a frown on her face. "Why did you do that?"

"Do what?"

"Act like you needed to come to my rescue. I could have handled that jerk. In fact, I was handling him just fine."

She was serious? She was mad at him? A smile pulled at his lips.

"Why are you laughing? This isn't funny."

"I'm not laughing. You just amaze me. You might not remember your past, but I can tell you that you are a very strong woman who doesn't take flak from anyone. I'm sorry I lost my head for a moment when I saw that guy touching you. I should have known you would handle the situation."

Her frown transformed into a smile. "You really think that about me?"

He stepped closer to her. "I do. Does this mean I'm out of trouble?"

"I suppose so."

"And how would you feel about me kissing you?"

Surprise reflected in her eyes. "I think I'd like it very much."

He reached out to her and drew her close. He lowered his head at the same time she lifted to her tiptoes. And then her lips were there beneath his. Oh, how he'd missed her sweetness.

The only thing he regretted was that they were in public and this kiss had to be brief. It was with the utmost restraint that he pulled away.

He stared into her eyes. "We'll pick this up later."

"I'll be waiting."

"Even if it's something casual? No strings attached."

"I think that would be perfect."

A smile tugged at the corners of his mouth. He was tired of pushing her away when it was so much better just to have some fun together. No strings would be spun between them. No expectations. Just something very enjoyable.

CHAPTER ELEVEN

ONE MORE ROOM CLEANED.

So many more to go.

A couple of days later, Cherie stepped into the hallway. A smile played on her lips. Antoine was responsible for it. Ever since they'd gone to the beach, things between them had changed for the better—a lot better.

They'd continued their talk about not getting serious. Neither of them knew what the future held when her memory returned. But secretly, she was certain nothing she learned about herself would change this thing that was growing between them.

And then they'd made mad, passionate love. Antoine was the most amazing lover. She would never forget their time together.

But perhaps they'd gotten a bit too rambunctious the last couple of nights, because today she was tired and her breasts were tender to the touch. Perhaps they'd have to be a bit gentler the next time. A smile pulled at her lips at the thought of spending another night with Antoine.

Right now, she needed to focus on cleaning this château. She couldn't help but think the château was something like a palace. There were just so many rooms.

She wondered if at some point in history this home had held a family so large that they filled all of the bedrooms. She shuddered at the thought of giving birth to that many children. She may have amnesia, but she was certain that with or without her memory, she wouldn't want to have that large of a family. But one or two babies that resembled Antoine would be nice. As soon as she realized the direction of her thoughts, she halted them. This thing with them was casual. Nothing more.

It was midmorning when Cherie finished cleaning another bedroom. With only an hour until Antoine would come in from the field for lunch, she decided she should get a head start on the next room.

The door was shut, unlike the other bedrooms doors that had been left ajar. When she turned the door handle and pushed, the door didn't open easily. It was as if it had been closed for so long that the hinges had rusted in place.

She gave a harder shove, and with a loud creak, the door gave way. As she stared in from the hallway, her first reaction to seeing the neglect in the room was that it would take her a very long time to make it presentable.

She pushed the door wide open. The sunlight streamed in through the gap in the faded drapes. The light caught on the massive cobwebs hanging from the chandelier in the center of the room. Cherie cringed. She could only hope the spiders that had spun them were long gone because those must have been some giant spiders. She inwardly shuddered.

Her gaze moved over the large chunky furniture. A large four-poster bed occupied the center of the room. It was painted white, like much of the other furniture. There was tulle wrapped loosely around the upper frame. It was hard to tell through the thick dust, but Cherie surmised that at one point the material might have been pink.

This must be Antoine's mother's room, she thought. Cherie wasn't sure what to do. Should she go out and close the door behind her? It was awkward being in here, knowing this room had been kept in honor of his mother.

But it didn't look like anyone had visited it in years. The painted white wood was covered in a thick layer of dust. While the other rooms had looked as though they hadn't been cleaned in a couple of years, this room looked as though it had been neglected for a couple of decades. It desperately needed someone to care for it.

And so she did what she did with all of the other rooms and started by the door, then worked counterclockwise around the room. As she worked, she noticed that this room, unlike the others, had newer furniture—all except one piece.

She stopped in front of an old antique desk. It was made of dark wood while the rest of the furniture was painted white. She wondered what was special about this desk that it had been chosen to be put in this room. It certainly stood out and not in a good way. On its own, the desk was charming, but placed with so much white, it just stood out.

The desk rested beneath a window that looked out over the rows of vines. Cherie knew if she sat at the desk, she would stare out the window and do more daydreaming than work.

She started at the top of the closed rolltop desk. She began dusting it, then she rolled back the top to find lots of small drawers and letter slots. If someone was into antiques, this would definitely impress them.

The desk was filled with colored pens and stationery with a sky-blue background, puffy white clouds and a rainbow. The drawers held little trinkets such as key rings and jewelry. It looked like the desk belonged to a young woman full of life and it had been left exactly as it had been when she'd last used it.

It seemed the desk meant a lot to her, as there were all kinds of treasures stashed in it. Cherie wondered if Antoine had searched it for a clue as to the identity of his father. As soon as the thought came to her, she dismissed it. Of course, he had. He'd probably searched the entire room.

But how could a young woman have a secret beau and not leave a trace of him in her room. Cherie had a feeling that Antoine's parents wouldn't have approved of the young man and that's why she kept his identity a secret.

Cherie took her time cleaning the desk. There were many intricate carvings that took time to clean. She really had to work to get the cloth in some of the corners. She even placed a pencil inside the cloth to clean some of the narrow grooves.

She had cleaned most of the desk when she reached the bottom left corner. It looked like two little drawers stacked on top of each other, but they wouldn't open. How strange. She wondered if they weren't supposed to open, or if somehow they'd been glued shut.

As she continued to clean, she used both hands to work her way through all of the little drawers. Her hand accidentally pushed on one of the letter dividers and suddenly the two little drawers that were stuck now opened. It was like they were a disguised cubbyhole.

She gasped. Had she just found a hidden compartment? Excitement flooded her veins. She bent over to find the hidden compartment filled with letters. Could they be letters from Antoine's father?

"Cherie?" Antoine's voice echoed down the hallway. "Lunchtime."

She didn't want to eat. She wanted to stay here and investigate the desk further. What other secrets did it contain? But first, she had to go get Antoine.

At last, it was lunchtime.

Antoine entered through the kitchen door. He'd already kicked off his boots outside. He couldn't remember ever being so eager for the midday meal, but now that Cherie had moved in, everything had changed. While his men were making do with their packed lunches, he couldn't resist slipping home.

He'd expected to find Cherie in the kitchen. Sometimes she had lunch waiting for him and sometimes they prepared lunch together. He didn't mind helping. After all, he just wanted to spend time with her.

"Cherie?"

He started down the hallway and then went up the staircase. He recalled her mentioning that she was working on the bedrooms that week. Just as he reached the landing, she came rushing toward him. Her eyes lit up as she came to a stop in front of him. A smile tugged at his lips. It was nice to see that she was as excited about seeing him as he was about seeing her.

"And how was your morning?" he asked.

"I found something. You have to come see." She took his hand in hers and led him back the hallway. Where was she taking him? And what exactly had she found to have her this excited?

They passed room after room until they reached the end of the hall. Then she approached what had been his mother's room.

He swallowed hard. He wasn't sure he was ready to face the ghosts that lurked in that room.

He stopped in the hallway. "I don't want to go in there."

"I understand. But I promise you it'll be worth it."

He didn't want to go in and remember the past. The walk down memory lane would ruin his mood and he was so happy now that they'd come to an agreement to have a no-commitment fling. Last night had been mind-blowing. But this talk of the past was putting a damper on his mood.

He shook his head. "I don't think so."

"Even if I told you that I found a secret compartment holding your mother's correspondence?"

That was a totally different story. "Show me."

She guided him over to the antique desk. This desk was such an anomaly. He never understood why his mother had it. It matched nothing in the room.

Cherie pointed to a drawer. "See that."

He reached out and grasped the drawer. It didn't budge. "I remember this drawer and the one below it. I tried to open them in the past. They won't budge. So I figured they were just decorative."

"I thought so, too, but then I did this." She pushed on one of the letter dividers. It didn't move. "I don't understand. I swear it moves." She tried again. "Why won't it work?"

"Here, let me try." He reached out and pushed on it, but nothing happened.

"This makes no sense. I just had it open when I was cleaning."

"Can you re-create what you were doing at the time?"

"I don't know. I can try." She reached for a dust rag and inserted a pencil in it. "Let's see." She pressed the rag against some of the trim. "No, that wasn't it. Wait. I was working on the corner. I was having a hard time getting the dust out of the corner. And when I leaned forward, my hand must have rested on the letter divider. Like this."

And just like that, the divider slid back and the little door sprang open. Antoine was in awe. Sure, he'd heard of old desks having secret compartments but he'd never seen one. And here his mother had owned one.

Cherie stepped aside and let him peer inside. There was a bundle of letters. He withdrew them. Only one was in an envelope. He checked the postage stamp. It was dated the year he was born.

His pulse raced as he grew excited that he'd finally found a link back to his father. The envelope was unopened. There was no name on the return address, just a location in Australia, but the ink was smeared. This was so much more than he ever had before.

He turned to Cherie. "Thank you."

"I didn't do anything. I was just cleaning. I hope those letters give you the answers you've been seeking."

"Let's go see." He pressed a kiss to her lips as though it was the most natural thing for him to do.

He took her hand in his and they headed back downstairs. He took a seat at the table while Cherie gathered some food for lunch, not that he had an appetite.

The letters were in chronological order and so he started with the oldest one. He read it aloud while Cherie warmed a couple bowls of soup in the new microwave he'd purchased.

These letters were definitely from his father. And it appeared they were in love. He was fascinated.

"So how do you suppose they met?" he said, pondering the question. "I mean, he was from Australia and my mother always lived in France."

"Maybe one of them went on holiday."

"It would have to have been my father because my grandfather didn't believe in holidays. He always said there was too much work to be done."

"But now that you've found the letters, maybe you'll be able to find the rest of the answers." Cherie placed a bowl of soup in front of him, as well as some sliced bread.

"I don't know. There's no name for my father. Just a *J*, or is that a *T*. Either way, it's a long way from a name. It seems like they were being careful so my grandfather wouldn't learn his identity."

"What do you think the secrecy was about?" Cherie carried over her own food and set it down beside Antoine.

"I don't know. But I could imagine my grandfather being overprotective, though I didn't experience it with me being a boy."

"Interesting." She glanced down at the table. "You have one last letter to read."

He reached for the unopened envelope. He hoped there were more clues to the identity of his father. He carefully opened it. He withdrew the letter and began to read.

Brigitte,
I'm so sorry I'm not there. You must be
so scared, being pregnant and alone. I
promise you that I'll be there as soon
as possible. I just need to take care of a
few last things here and then I'll be on
the next plane to you.

Antoine's gaze blurred. He blinked repeatedly, gathering his emotions. His father knew about him. So why hadn't he shown up? What had kept him from them?

I can't write for long. I have to go back
to work. But know that I'm thinking of
you and our little one.
I love you both so very much.
I'll see you soon,
J

A tear splashed onto the page. Antoine didn't realize how much he'd longed to hear those words. He was loved by his parents. They might not have been able to be in his life, but they'd loved him. It meant the world for him to know that.

He didn't trust his voice so he handed Cherie the letter to read for herself. While she perused the letter, he wondered if he'd been too hasty in writing off having a family of his own. His gaze drifted to Cherie. He imagined her with a baby—his baby.

The thought jarred him back to reality. He still didn't have the first clue how to be a good parent. The letters helped fill a void in him, but they didn't change his decision not to have children.

"What do you think happened to your father?" she asked.

"I don't know but I hope these letters will point me in the right direction. I have a private investigator in Paris. I want to show him this envelope and the letters to see if he can restart the investigation with them."

"You already had him search for your father?"

"I did, years ago. But there was so little information to go on that he wasn't able to come up with anything. Now that I know they were sneaking around, it explains so many things, like my grandfather not knowing who my father was." He turned to Cherie. "This means he didn't lie to me."

"No. He didn't."

His gaze met hers. "Thank you. If it weren't for you, I might never have found these letters."

"I'm glad I was able to help."

He excused himself and headed outside. He needed some fresh air—a chance to make sense of what he'd learned. And to put some space between him and Cherie. He had to be careful they didn't get too comfortable because he wasn't staying at the château forever.

His home—his life—was in Paris. And Cherie had another life—one she would hopefully remember any time now. And then they'd go their separate ways.

CHAPTER TWELVE

She awoke with a smile.

The next morning, Cherie stretched. It was her best night's sleep ever. Not that there was much sleep going on. Antoine had been in the best mood.

He had wrapped up his work early and insisted on taking her to dinner at a quaint restaurant in the village. She hadn't been about to argue. There would be plenty of time for her to clean the rest of the house later.

And as happy as she was for him finding some clues to his past, she was still in the dark when it came to her own memory. She was starting to wonder if they'd missed something in the scans she'd had done.

Part of her said maybe it was a good thing she couldn't recall her past because she might not like the person she'd once been. This was a chance for her to re-create herself any way she saw fit. The other part of her longed to know who her parents were and whether or not she had any siblings. She had a million questions about herself. What was her occupation? Where was her home? The questions were endless.

Knowing she couldn't lie around all day, she got out of Antoine's bed. There was work to be done. After making the bed, she grabbed a shower.

It was still very early in the morning. She was surprised that Antoine would already be out in the field working at that hour. She dressed and headed for the kitchen.

When she reached the entryway into the kitchen, a horrific stench stopped her in her tracks. What in the world was it? Cherie's stomach took a nauseous lurch.

Her mouth grew moist and she swallowed hard. With one hand, she clutched the doorframe and gazed about the kitchen, searching for the source of the smell.

Antoine glance up from the stove. A slow smile lifted his lips. "Good morning, sleepyhead. Come join me."

She didn't budge. "What did you make?"

"A cheese omelet and coffee."

Her stomach heaved. She pressed a hand to her midsection, struggling not to get sick right there. "Your eggs—they're rotten."

His eyebrows scrunched together. "No, they aren't. I just tasted them." Concern reflected in his eyes. "Are you alright?"

She didn't dare open her mouth. Instead, she turned on her heel and raced to the bathroom, slamming the door shut behind her. Her stomach emptied its contents.

A couple of minutes later, there was a knock at the door. She bid him entrance. She felt embarrassed for getting sick over the smell of the meal he'd cooked, but she couldn't understand how it didn't smell rotten to him.

He didn't say anything as he dampened a cloth and then joined her on the floor. He pressed the cloth to her forehead. The coldness felt very good against her warmed skin.

Once she felt a bit better, she said, "I'm sorry."

"It's okay." His voice was soft and gentle. "You must have picked up a bug somewhere along the way. Maybe it was at the hospital."

"The thing is, I don't feel sick. It was just the smell—it got to me."

"Has it ever happened before?" And then, as though he realized the error of his question, he asked, "I meant, has it happened since you've been here?"

She shook her head. Her body grew tense.

This wasn't the only thing that seemed odd to her. She recalled the tenderness of her breasts. It hadn't subsided. They were still very sore.

Then she realized she hadn't had her period since she'd awakened in the hospital. She gasped. Was it possible that she was late? It was so hard to tell with this amnesia.

"Cherie, what is it?"

She couldn't tell him what she was thinking. What if she was wrong? She would have worried him for nothing.

When she didn't respond, he asked again, "What is it? What are you thinking?"

Maybe she should tell him. After all, if she was pregnant she hadn't gotten in the situation all on her own. And there had been the accident with the condom that first night. They'd thought it'd torn after, but what if it had happened before or during their lovemaking?

"Cherie, you're worrying me?" He turned to her and gripped her shoulders. "Talk to me."

"I—I think I might be pregnant."

He immediately let go of her as though her words had physically shocked him—as if he couldn't get away from her fast enough. Instead of heading out the door as fast as his legs would carry him, he scooted a fair distance from her and leaned back against the wall. His eyes were wide open as he stared straight ahead. He wasn't alone in his shock. She had no idea how much time passed as they each struggled to come to terms with her potential pregnancy. When she was certain her nausea had passed, she got to her feet. She brushed her teeth. And then she grasped the doorknob, but then hesitated.

She didn't want to step out there and have the stench hit her again. She didn't want to go through that all over again.

"It's okay," Antoine said. "I already opened the door and windows before I came in here. It should be aired out by now. If you want, I'll go first and check."

She was tempted to let him lead the way, but she refused to back down, certainly not over some stench. She was stronger than that—she'd have to be if she was pregnant.

Pregnant. The word echoed in her mind. *This can't be possible. Surely not.*

She stepped out of the bathroom, prepared for a wave of rotten eggs, but the stench was gone. Thank goodness.

She didn't know where to go or what to do. At the moment, she felt as though the world had tilted and she was struggling to regain her footing.

A potential pregnancy couldn't have happened at a worse time. Her memory hadn't returned yet. She didn't know if it ever would. And Antoine was only ever meant to be a brief fling—not a co-parent. Not that he would co-parent with her, because he'd already told her that he never wanted to be a father.

Her shoulders dropped. The world felt as though it was crashing down upon her. She would be all alone, with no family, no support system and no source of income other than what Antoine had offered her for cleaning the château.

She glanced over at Antoine. He was on the other side of the living room. The yawning gap between them had never felt so large. In that moment, she'd never felt so alone.

A part of her wanted to pretend that the last hour hadn't happened—that she could go back to being blissfully ignorant of the fact she could be carrying Antoine's baby. But that wasn't possible. They had to find out right away if she was pregnant.

The tests were in a brown paper bag.

It rested on the passenger seat and kept drawing Antoine's attention. He couldn't believe that he…um, *they* were in this situation.

Was she pregnant? And if she was, what happened next?

He had no answers. It's part of the reason he'd volunteered to go get a pregnancy test—a couple of them, just to be sure. But he didn't go into the village for the purchase. In the past few months that he'd been working on the vineyard, he'd become reacquainted with many people in the small village. The last thing he wanted was to stir up gossip by purchasing a pregnancy test.

And so he decided to drive into Saint-Tropez—someplace where he wouldn't know the salesclerk. He welcomed the drive. He thought some time alone would give him some clarity, but he was more confused now than ever.

He'd taken great pains in the past to make certain he was never put in this position. But with Cherie, he had let down his guard. He'd let passion take over and mistakes had been made. What was it about Cherie that had him doing things he'd never done before?

He pulled to a stop outside the château. He sat there in the car for a moment, gathering his thoughts. He had to keep it together. After all, it was more likely that she wasn't pregnant. The thought still didn't help him relax.

He drew in a deep breath and then blew it

out. And then he repeated it. This is as calm as he was going to get until he knew the results of the test.

On shaky legs, he headed inside. Cherie practically met him at the door. Without a word, he held the bag out to her. She took it and started back down the hallway. He followed. At the bathroom doorway, she frowned at him.

He suddenly realized what he was doing. "I'll, uh, wait for you in the living room."

He retraced his steps to the foyer and then turned to enter the living room, but he was in no shape to sit still, so he started pacing. All the while, he willed the test result to be negative.

His neck hurt and his shoulders ached. A throbbing started in his forehead. When his phone buzzed, he ignored it. Nothing mattered in this moment except the result of that test.

He paced from the doorway of the living room to the grand fireplace. When he turned around, Cherie was standing there. There were unshed tears in her eyes. He couldn't tell if they were tears of joy or despair.

When she didn't speak, he started toward her. She held the test out to him. It wasn't until he lifted his hand to take it from her that he noticed the slight tremor in his fingers.

Everything seemed to move in slow motion. He recognized the enormity of this moment. Either his life could return to the way it had been, with him preparing to sell this vineyard and return to his business in Paris, or his life would be forever changed in ways that he hadn't even contemplated yet.

He lifted the test strip and looked at the little window. He blinked because he wasn't sure he was seeing it correctly. But then he opened his eyes and focused on the white strip. It had the same answer.

Pregnant.

He stared at it for a moment, as though reading the word over and over again would help it settle in his mind. It didn't work. This couldn't be right.

His gaze lifted to meet Cherie's. "Are you sure?"

She held out the second test. He didn't want to take it. He didn't want confirmation of what he already knew. And yet, there was this tiny hope that the test would read negative.

He accepted the second test. It had the same answer as the first one.

He was going to be a father. *A father.*

Fatherhood was the one thing he knew

nothing about. How in the world was he supposed to be a good parent when he'd never had one? The questions and doubts came one after the other.

He retreated until the backs of his knees struck the couch. He dropped down on it. He tossed the strips onto the coffee table. His elbows rested on his knees as he rested his face in his hands. What were they going to do now?

When he started to think of it from a more analytical mindset, he was better able to function. He glanced over at Cherie, who was sitting in a window seat, staring outside. With her head turned away from him, he wasn't able to see what she might be thinking.

He didn't imagine she was coping any better than him. After all, she didn't even know the name given to her at birth. She didn't know who her parents were, much less if they were good parents or not.

It was imperative now that she got her memory back as soon as possible. There had to be more they could do than just sit around and wait. As far as he could tell, that wasn't doing anything to help her.

"When I get my memory back, everything is going to change for us."

The statement was like a crescendo in the

quiet room. The truth of her words weighed on him. What would happen when she remembered her past? Would she still want to continue this, whatever their relationship could be called?

Antoine cleared his throat. "I think we should go to Paris."

She turned. Her eyebrows were knit together with confusion. "What's in Paris?"

"Specialists. We've waited for your memory to return on its own. Now it's time to consult a specialist and see if there's something more they can do to help things along. What do you think?"

She was quiet for a moment, as though considering his suggestion, and then she nodded. "Let's do it."

"And while we're there we can see a doctor about your pregnancy. To make sure you and the baby are fine."

She nodded again.

At least she wasn't fighting him or putting up demands. He appreciated her not pushing him for answers because he had none. He needed time to come to terms with the fact that he was about to become a father. It was a position he never anticipated he'd end up in.

CHAPTER THIRTEEN

HER BRAIN SCANS were negative.

Her official pregnancy test was positive.

Two days ago, she'd met with a neurologist that Antoine had arranged for her to see. She was impressed with how quickly they'd squeezed her in. They'd said they had a cancellation, but she couldn't help wondering if that was the truth, or if Antoine had used his connections and called in a favor. She wouldn't put it past him, as she'd never seen him look so worried.

He'd stayed with her all day as she had one test after the next. The neurologist wasn't leaving anything unchecked. The wait time to take the tests was lengthy. But she didn't complain, because she had been so grateful they had fit her into their busy schedule.

Antoine had gone out of his way to entertain her so she wouldn't stress. She had been concerned there would be some sort of permanent damage that would keep her memories from her. She worried that even if they located her family, she wouldn't be able to remember them.

And then yesterday afternoon, she'd had an obstetrics appointment. It went a lot faster than her neurology appointment. She was told everything appeared to be on track with her pregnancy. Though they did caution her that the first trimester was the riskiest, and since she couldn't remember her medical history, they would remain cautiously optimistic.

Yesterday evening, they'd met with Antoine's private investigator, who wasn't overly exuberant with the letter they'd uncovered, since part of the return address was smudged. He didn't say it was hopeless—instead, he said he'd work on it. She could tell the investigator's lack of enthusiasm was a downer to Antoine, but she refused to let him give up. There might not be a name, and part of the address might be illegible, but they had a general location. It was a lot more than he had before.

Through it all, she'd been focused on the future. She didn't know how, but she was certain it was all going to work out—her memory would come back and Antoine would unlock the secrets of his past. All she had now was hope and a baby counting on her to figure it all out. She refused to let down their baby.

She already knew that no matter what, she was keeping the baby. She felt an instant bond to little Antoine or little Cherie. She couldn't wait to hold them in her arms.

She made concerted efforts to remember her past. It was what she concentrated on when she went to bed alone and the first thing she thought of when she awoke alone. Nothing she did seemed to help.

Antoine had been there with her through it all, but he might as well have not been there because he didn't talk to her. Ever since they'd discovered she was pregnant, it was like a wall had gone up between them. She told him that it was fine if he wanted to go to his office to get some work done, but he stubbornly refused.

That morning, she couldn't take his gloomy attitude any longer, so she insisted he go to the office for a while. They weren't doing each other any good being together. The tension between them was so thick that they couldn't talk about the most inconsequential things, such as what to eat without a disagreement.

While he was away, she went for a walk. She hoped something in this amazingly beautiful city would jar a memory—that it would open a floodgate. Because she instinctively felt at home in Paris. She couldn't recall anything specific, but she knew deep down in her bones that this city was filled with good memories for her. If only she could grasp those elusive memories.

She walked and walked, all the while lost in her thoughts. She found she loved browsing through the many boutiques. She loved clothes. Not just buying them, but she would pick up a skirt and think of how she could improve it. Was that some sort of memory? She had no idea, but she definitely felt like she was getting closer to remembering her past.

When she came upon a particularly colorful boutique window, it drew her in. She paused to take a closer look at the pastel pink skirt with small white flowers and lime-green leaves.

She noticed the way the material was gathered at the waistline, giving the skirt movement. She took in the color of the thread in the seams. And she liked how the skirt was designed to fall a few centimeters above the knee, not too high and not too low.

It wasn't the desire to wear the skirt that drew her to it. It was the way the skirt was crafted. She wondered if she had the right materials, if she could create a similar skirt. Wait. Did that mean she was a seamstress?

She felt as though she was on a precipice and her memories were just out of reach. She turned and started to walk again. If she kept moving, if she kept filling her mind with images, she was going to remember her life. She was certain of it.

Buzz-buzz.

The phone Antoine had given her rang. She withdrew it from the little inexpensive purse that she'd picked up in the village near the château. The caller ID said it was Antoine. She wasn't sure she was ready to speak to him yet.

She was on the verge of something— something big. She worried the stress of dealing with him would distract her and ruin her ability to recall her past. And this baby was counting on her to figure things out—to be able to provide for it and give it a loving home.

And yet if she didn't answer the phone, she knew Antoine would worry that she'd gotten lost or something had happened to her. It was best just to answer the phone and let him know she was alright. A quick conversation and then she could continue to make her way through Paris, searching for her past.

She pressed the phone to her ear. "Hello."

"I'm still at the office. Where are you?"

"Walking."

"Still?" His voice was filled with disbelief. "It's been a few hours."

"I know. There's just something about this city. I feel like I know it."

"What does that mean? Is your memory coming back?"

"It's nothing specific. I just get the feeling I've been here before."

"That's good. Right?"

"I think so."

"But you need to eat. Let's grab some lunch."

Was it that late already? She checked the time on her phone. It was time to eat, but she wasn't ready to stop exploring this magical city. "I'm fine. I'll grab something later."

"Let's do it together. Where are you?"

She hesitated. She knew once she saw him—once the questions and uncertainty about her future were dredged up—that she would lose this chance to latch on to the memories that were just out of her reach.

"Cherie, what's going on? Why don't you want me to know where you are?" Agitation laced the edge of his voice. "Are you purposely avoiding me?"

Guilt assailed her. She'd been upset when he'd put a wall up between them, and now she was doing it to him. They were going to be parents. They had to learn how to deal with each other through the good and the troubling times.

She told him the name of the intersection. She glanced around and noticed a small café nearby. It offered indoor and outdoor dining. It looked inviting.

He promised to meet her at the café in a matter of minutes.

As she made her way across the street, she realized that the time was coming when they would need to have a very frank conversation about the baby and their future. She wasn't looking forward to it.

He was worried about her.

Antoine got up from behind the desk in his Paris office. A lot of work had piled up since he'd been gone. It would take him weeks to get caught up on everything.

But his heart wasn't in his work. He was distracted with thoughts of Cherie and the baby. He still couldn't believe they were going to be parents. *Parents*.

He exited his office without saying a word to his assistant. He was lost in his thoughts.

Cherie hadn't been her normal cheerful self since learning the news of her pregnancy. Not that he could blame her. He was still struggling with the reality of the situation.

He hadn't wanted to leave Cherie that morning. She'd insisted that she needed some time alone. And there was the fact that he'd been neglecting his business for far too long. He knew he had to make a decision about where his future lay—in Saint-Tropez working the vineyard, or here in Paris running his import business.

Because both jobs were demanding. And there just wasn't enough time in the day to care for both businesses. A difficult choice must be made: keep running the business he'd started from scratch years ago, or return to his roots in the south of France?

He knew which way he was leaning and it scared him. There was just something about working with the soil, the fresh air and being outside all day in the warm sunshine that called to him. In his haste to get away from his grandfather, he'd forgotten just how much he enjoyed the vineyard.

But was it truly the vineyard that he enjoyed? Or was it Cherie's company at the château that made it so comfortable? He wondered what would happen when her memory returned. Would she want to stay with him? Or would she want to take the baby and return to her other life?

His finger stabbed at the elevator button. So far, nothing about his return to Paris had gone as he'd planned. His meeting the prior evening with his investigator hadn't been promising. The investigator remained guarded about his ability to track down Antoine's father even with the aid of the letters Cherie had found.

He stepped onto the elevator. Antoine felt a deep desperation to find his father—to ask him why he had changed his mind and abandoned him. If he could get those answers, maybe it would help him navigate his journey in parenthood.

Though the address hadn't been fully legible, it still had a location in Australia. That clue was big. It was so much more than they had before.

Antoine didn't care if he had to go to Australia personally. He was going to take this clue as far as it would go. In fact, he liked the idea of traveling to Australia with his investigator. They could cover twice as much ground, twice as fast. But all of that was for another day.

A few minutes later, Antoine arrived at the

café. Cherie was standing out front waiting for him. She didn't smile when she saw him. With her dark sunglasses on, he was unable to see her eyes to know what she was thinking.

She suggested they take a table outside. It was a beautiful day, with a blue sky and hardly a cloud in sight. It wasn't too warm or too cool. And he realized they'd be away from any aromas that might turn her stomach. Although he was starting to notice how her stomach bothered her more in the morning and then settled by lunchtime. He hoped the morning sickness didn't last her entire pregnancy.

When Antoine spoke, it was in a soft tone because he didn't want anyone to overhear their conversation. "So you've been walking all morning?" When she nodded, he asked, "Are you sure that's good for the baby? Maybe you should be resting."

"Antoine, the doctor didn't say anything about resting. The baby is fine."

"Shh…" He glanced around. "Let's not make the information public."

"I'm not making anything public."

Her lips pressed together into a firm line. He was still unable to look into her eyes for a hint as to what she was thinking because she still had on those big, dark sunglasses.

"Can you take those off?" He gestured to her glasses.

She hesitated at first, but then slid them off and placed them in her purse. When her gaze met his, there was a definite frown on her face.

The server stopped at their table to take their order. Antoine ordered a sandwich. He noticed how Cherie hesitated and he wondered if her stomach was still bothering her. She finally ordered some soup.

When they were alone again, Antoine rested his elbows on the table and leaned toward her. "I think after lunch we should go back to the château, where we can talk privately."

"I'm not ready to go back. Not yet."

He got the feeling she wanted to avoid him. "What are you going to do here? You can't just keep walking around hoping you'll see something to spark your memory." He whispered, "We have to talk about an arrangement for…you know."

"The baby." Her voice was loud and clear.

His body tensed. "Shh…"

"Don't shush me!" She glared at him.

He noticed a couple of women at a nearby table turning and glancing at her. They didn't outright ogle them, like a man nearby was doing, but he could still feel their periodic glances.

"Do you know those women over there?" Cherie nodded toward them. "They seem very interested in us."

He glanced over at them. When one lady looked his way, he glowered at her. The woman's face turned three shades of red and she turned away.

He turned his attention back Cherie. "No, I don't. Some people are just nosy."

Even so, it was awkward having strangers staring at them and whispering about them. Maybe coming here hadn't been such a good idea.

Her gaze met his. "Let's leave."

"No. We haven't eaten. You need to eat for…" His voice trailed away as his gaze lowered to her midsection.

She lowered her voice when she said, "I'm not going to whisper and keep this all a secret."

"We need some privacy while we figure this out."

"No, we don't." Her voice rose in frustration.

"Cherie, be reasonable."

She stared directly at him as she asked in

hushed tone, "What do you want to do about the baby?"

He didn't say a word for a long time. When she implored him with her eyes, he said, "I don't know."

"I've lost my appetite." Her chair scraped over the concrete as she got to her feet.

"Cherie, wait." He dropped some money on the table.

"No, Antoine. I just need some time alone."

He stepped up next to her. "Let's go back to the apartment."

"I..." Now all eyes were openly staring at them. "Alright. Let's go."

More and more people stared at them. It wasn't even like they'd had a big, blowout argument or anything. So why was everyone staring at them?

CHAPTER FOURTEEN

Cherie wanted answers.

And he had none to give her.

Antoine wasn't used to being in this position. Usually he was the one who knew the answers, led the charge, found the solutions. And now he felt at a complete loss.

How was he supposed be a good father when he'd never even met his own? Honestly, he didn't even know how to hold a baby. He'd never done it in his life. Now he was about to be a father and he felt like everything was spinning out of control. Even his search to find his father was dubious at best.

How were either of them supposed to be good parents when he didn't know what it was like to have one and she couldn't remember hers? This whole situation was a mess.

Antoine paced back and forth in his modernly decorated living room with light gray walls and black leather couches. The walls lacked any decorations. He didn't have an artistic flair and there was no one in his life he wanted picking out the décor for his home— at least before Cherie had stepped into his life.

He'd tried sitting down but he couldn't stay still. He knew what the right thing to do was, but he wasn't ready to get married. Just the thought made his gut knot up. He didn't know if he'd ever be ready for that sort of commitment.

Maybe if he was a bigger man or had a more conventional upbringing, he would propose to her. It might not be a romantic union, but they were compatible in and out of bed, although he just couldn't bring himself to promise Cherie forever. He would feel trapped. That was no way to begin a long-term relationship. It wouldn't be fair to either of them and especially not the baby.

"I thought we came here to talk." Cherie was perched on the edge of one couch. "So far you haven't said a word."

He raked his fingers through his hair. "I won't be pressured into a commitment."

"What?" She jumped to her feet.

"You heard me. I'm not proposing or anything like that so don't even think about it."

Her eyebrows drew together as her eyes

shot daggers at him. "Trust me, the thought hadn't even crossed my mind."

"It's for the best." He didn't want to do anything to hurt her. And leaping into a committed relationship right now would lead to a disaster, especially when she got her memory back.

"So what you're saying is now that I'm pregnant, I'm on my own."

He hadn't said that. And it wasn't what he meant. "That's not what I'm saying."

She stared at him with disbelief in her eyes. "What are you saying?"

"I don't know. I wasn't planning on having a family so I never thought about what I'd do if it happened. I just know I can't give you the family you want and deserve. I can get you all set up with an apartment here in Paris. I'll make sure you and the baby are financially provided for."

"Don't bother. You don't have to worry about me." She turned and headed for the door.

He was hot on her heels. "Cherie, where are you going?"

"Out. Don't follow me. I need time." She opened the door and rushed out, letting the door slam shut behind her.

He stood there staring at the closed door.

That hadn't gone well, not well at all. He knew he should go after her. He should apologize for not being able to give her the security of a loving and caring relationship. He needed to reassure her that he would always support her and the baby.

And yet he hesitated. Cherie was sweet and thoughtful. She deserved so much better than him. He was broken on the inside.

He needed to explain this to her. She needed to understand his avoidance of a relationship wasn't about her—it was all about him.

He took off, out the door. He skipped the elevator and rushed to the stairs. He raced down the steps. He caught sight of Cherie as she walked out the door into a sea of camera flashes. What in the world?

He didn't want her.

And he didn't want their baby.

Cherie rode the elevator down to the ground floor. She swiped away the unwanted tears. She needed to put space between them before something was said that neither of them could take back. Because whether she liked it or not, they had to find a way to get along for their child.

Luckily, their baby hadn't been born yet, because she wasn't ready to be mature and cooperative at the moment. Right now, she was upset with Antoine for jumping to conclusions—for him assuming she wanted to marry him. She didn't even know her own name, so how was she supposed to know whom she wanted to spend the rest of her life with?

If only she could remember her life, she would have choices—she could plan a life for her baby.

Think. Think. Think.

She closed her eyes and concentrated so hard that her temples started to throb.

Who are my parents? Where do I live? What is my name?

The elevator dinged and the door slid open. Her eyelids fluttered open. The glass doors were across the marbled foyer from her— her escape.

She didn't have a destination. She just couldn't go back upstairs. Not yet. She needed to calm down and work on getting her memories back.

She stepped out of the elevator. As she neared the front doors, she noticed a bunch of people standing out on the sidewalk. What was going on? Did someone famous live in the building?

She pushed through the first set of doors and then the second. A warm summer breeze rushed over her face right before everything spun out of control.

The next thing she knew there was a camera in her face. A flash blinded her. Suddenly there was an endless series of flashes going off in her face. They momentarily blinded her. The flashes were like lightbulbs going off in her mind.

It was then that she had a flashback. In that moment, it was as if time slowed down. She was all dressed up at the opera house and there were paparazzi all around her. They were taking her photo and asking her questions, just as they were doing now.

And then her memories took on a sharper focus. In her mind's eye, she saw herself pass in front of a mirrored wall on her way to a waiting car. She was wearing a formal blue-and-silver gown. And on her head was a tiara.

She gasped! She knew who she was—she was Her Royal Highness Princess Cecelia of Rydiania. She was royalty.

The past and present collided. She struggled to keep her balance as her world toppled sideways. In her mind, she struggled to make sense of everything she remembered.

She was not a housekeeper.

She was the daughter of the king and queen of Rydiania, a small European country.

She had an older brother and two sisters.

Piece by piece, her life was coming together like a jigsaw puzzle. How could she have forgotten all of that? How could she have forgotten herself?

The other details of her life were still a bit vague, like why she had been in France at the time of her accident, but she was certain it would come to her. If she just had some time to herself, she was certain she could fill in the remaining gaps in her memory.

And then, time fast-forwarded, leaving her in the center of this chaos.

"Princess Cecelia! Princess Cecelia!" The reporters kept calling out her name.

She knew her birth name. Cecelia. Princess Cecelia. Happy, relieved tears rushed to her eyes, but she quickly blinked them away. Celebrating would have to wait. She instinctively knew to keep her emotions under wraps in front of the press.

Right now, she stood in the middle of a sea of paparazzi. They were all yelling questions at her. She needed to get away from them. She needed to get to the Rydianian embassy. It was finally time to go home.

Home. It sounded so good.

As she tried to work her way through the crowd, she made her way to the curb. A dark

SUV rolled up. The doors opened and two big burly men with short haircuts, dark sunglasses and charcoal suits jumped out and rushed to her. They pushed back the crowd.

"Your Royal Highness, come with us," the man with an earpiece said to her.

She couldn't put names to them, but she recognized them. She instinctively knew that she was safe with them. And so she moved quickly to the SUV. She was ushered inside. All the while, the paparazzi kept calling out to her.

"What are you doing in Paris?"

"Who were you meeting?"

"Does your family know where you are?"

The door closed and the tinted windows gave her a modicum of privacy. The reporters pressed against the SUV like a bunch of crazed fans. She ducked her head and shielded her face with her hands.

All of a sudden, she missed the anonymity the persona of Cherie had allowed her. She distinctly remembered her dislike of being in the spotlight—of having cameras pointed at her, of having microphones shoved in her face.

The SUV slowly navigated through the throng of reporters. And then they were on their way. At last, she could breathe easy.

"Package safe," the bodyguard in the front

seat said into his communications device. "En route."

"Where are we going?" Cecelia asked.

"To the airport, Your Royal Highness. The queen has asked to have you returned to the palace ASAP."

"How did you find me?"

"We tracked you as far as the airport, but then we lost track of you, ma'am. It wasn't until a little earlier that you were spotted on social media here in Paris."

"Social media? What were they saying?"

"I'm not sure, Your Highness."

She knew he was dodging her question. She reached for her phone, but then recalled that she'd been so upset with Antoine that she'd forgotten the phone he'd given her.

Antoine. What would she tell him? How could she even begin to explain? What would this mean for them? For the baby. But then he didn't really want her or the baby, did he?

"My phone was stolen. I'll have to get another one."

"We already have one ready for you." The bodyguard held a phone out to her.

She turned it on and immediately pulled up a tabloid site. Missing Princess Has New Look! And then there was a photo of her at the café with her new blond hairstyle.

CHAPTER FIFTEEN

WHAT WAS GOING ON?

Antoine rushed after Cherie. He saw her pass through the glass doors. He watched as she became engulfed by the crowd outside. Where had all of these people come from? There was never such a large gathering in front of his apartment building. Had there been an accident or death?

All he wanted was to reach Cherie and keep her safe. He pushed open the exterior door just in time to see some large man in a dark suit step up to Cherie. The man ushered her toward a big dark SUV.

"Cherie!" His voice got lost in the yelling of the crowd. "Cherie, stop!"

He tried to reach her but his efforts were hampered by the crowd. He refused to let anyone stand between him and Cherie. He pushed. He shoved. He elbowed his way toward the road, toward the SUV, toward Cherie.

And he reached it just as it pulled away. His hand landed on the rear corner panel for the briefest second before the vehicle swiftly sped off.

He ran after it, but he soon realized they weren't going to stop. Who in the world had taken Cherie? Had she been kidnapped?

He turned around. The paparazzi ran up to him. They stuck their phones in his face.

"How do you know the princess?"

"Has Princess Cecelia been staying with you?"

Princess?

Princess Cecelia?

The power of those words had Antoine stepping back as he attempted to take in the enormity of what the reporters were telling him. But it just seemed too far-fetched, too over-the-top. And yet they seemed so certain.

Princess? The word stuck in his mind. Cherie was Princess Cecelia? The knot in his gut returned. This would teach him for not paying attention to social media.

And now, in a blink of an eye, their once idyllic situation had changed once more. Everything had become infinitely more complicated.

He had things he wanted to ask her. There were important matters they had to sort out.

But most of all, he realized he wasn't ready for her to just be gone. He didn't like the possibility of not seeing her again. And with her being a princess of a foreign country, the rules had all changed.

As much as he wanted things to go back to the way they had once been, he knew that moment had long passed them. Cherie... erm, Princess Cecelia would be returning to her family. How would they feel when they learned about the baby?

Would they try to keep them apart? The thought of being permanently separated from his own child created a fiercely protective instinct in him. No one would stand between them. He didn't care what he had to do.

Was this what it felt like to be a parent? Was this how his own parents had felt? Because right now he was willing to go to the ends of the earth for Cecelia and their baby. Maybe being a parent wasn't all learned— maybe some of it was instinctual. Could that be?

A reporter's voice drew him from his thoughts. "Can you tell us how you know the princess?"

"Are you the princess's boyfriend?"

He once again pushed his way through the crowd, while they continued to bombard him with questions about the princess. He continued to ignore them.

Using his key card, he gained entrance to the apartment building. He'd never been so grateful for the building's security as he was right now.

Once he was back in his apartment, he reached for his phone. His fingers moved rapidly over the screen as he typed a message.

Are you okay?

As soon as he sent the message, there was a buzz. He glanced at the coffee table to find that she'd left her phone behind. Intentionally? He didn't think so.

He remembered how upset she'd been when she'd rushed out the door. She was angry at him because he couldn't say all of the loving words of devotion she'd wanted to hear. But he refused to lie to her—to tell her that he was ready for an instant family. He was still struggling with the idea of being a good father.

Now that Cecelia was gone, his apartment felt so empty. He sunk down on the couch and did a search on his phone. He typed *Princess Cecelia* into the search engine.

The first thing he noticed in the older photos was her long golden-brown curls. The style was quite different from the very short blond hairdo that Cherie wore. If this was her, what would drive her to cut off her hair and bleach it?

He continued to peruse the photos. This woman had the same pert nose and high cheekbones. He enlarged the photo, taking in the woman's enchanting blue eyes. And then there were her pouty lips, as well as the dimples in her cheeks.

It was her!

His Cherie was really Princess Cecelia.

He was so relieved that she had found her past, her family. He wondered if her memory had returned also. He wanted to ask her, but with the phone he'd gotten her still at the apartment, he had no way to reach her. He wanted to tell her that he was happy for her—no one should lose their past.

As quickly as his joy over her finding herself came to him, in the next heartbeat his heart sank. If he'd been worried about losing her before, when her memory came back, he was extremely worried now. He'd had a royal princess cleaning his house. He inwardly groaned. She was never ever going to want to see him again after the way he'd mistaken her for a housekeeper. It was no wonder she didn't seem to have a clue about cleaning.

In her other world, she probably had a small army of cleaning staff to keep her palace all neat and tidy. He was quite certain that until the day their lives had collided, she'd never run a vacuum or used a dustrag.

He felt like such an idiot. How could he have not known that there was something special about her? Well, he had noticed her specialness, but he had no idea she had royal blood.

This revelation put a kink in things. He'd wanted her to stay here with him—to continue this thing that they'd started, to see where it would go. Maybe one day it would have led to marriage. Now he'd never know. Unless he went after her...

Home at last.

Now that her memories were returning, Cecelia recalled the tension at the palace and her breakup with Paul. It all seemed so far away now. The broken heart she'd thought she'd had when Paul broke up with her, she now realized wasn't a broken heart. It was fear.

Fear that she'd never find the right person. Fear that the paparazzi would ruin any chance she would have at happiness. Fear that no one would love her enough to put up with her complicated life.

Those fears hadn't gone away since meeting Antoine. If anything, he'd only confirmed her reasons to worry.

Cecelia had had the embassy send word to Antoine that she was safe and returning to Rydiania. She had been given fresh clothes—clothes befitting a princess. And now she sat all alone in the rear seat of the plane. She told herself that she should be relieved to be going home. She no longer had to rely on Antoine's generosity.

Her memory was back for the most part. There were still a few gray areas, but she was certain with a little more time her memory would be crystal-clear.

But there was a part of her that felt betrayed by Antoine. He'd been all into her when things were light and fun. Now that things had gotten complicated and there was a baby involved, he was pushing her away with both hands. It hurt. It hurt so much.

Had she only imagined there had been something growing between them? She hadn't thought so at the time, but looking back on their weeks together, he'd made certain she knew he didn't do commitment. The painful truth was he felt nothing for her. And the best thing she could do for herself and the baby was to put him behind her. It shouldn't be too hard, considering he didn't want her... or their baby.

Now exhausted and heartbroken, she'd undoubtedly have to face her mother, who would be very unhappy about her escapade and the ensuing press coverage. Hopefully, her father would be happy to see her. He always left problems with Cecelia and her sisters up to their mother. For Cecelia, it meant having to deal with only one parent instead of both of them at once.

In the darkness of night, the plane touched down in Rydiania. Camera flashes lit up the night as her chauffeured car was ushered from the tarmac and through the gate to the main road. All the while, her thoughts returned to Antoine. She wondered what he was doing now. Was he relieved to know she was gone?

The answers she conjured up made her even more miserable. She stared out into the inky black night as her hand moved to her still flat midsection.

Don't worry, baby, you'll always have me.

All too soon, they were on palace grounds. At least it was late at night. Hopefully, she could slip away to her bed chamber without having to answer any questions.

But as she stepped inside the palace, she was greeted by her mother's private secretary. The older woman's eyes widened at the sight of her. Cecelia had forgotten about her radical hair change. Her hand moved to her hair, hoping it wasn't messed up from slumbering on the plane. She'd had her hair short for long enough now that she was used to it, but no one in the palace had seen her new look.

In the blink of an eye, the woman's expression resumed a neutral expression. "Your Highness, the queen is waiting for you in her office."

Cecelia inwardly groaned. So much for not answering any questions. "Thank you."

She didn't want to face her mother, but she wasn't going to avoid her, either. It was best to get this over as quickly as she could. It was quite possible that her father would be waiting to speak with her as well. But then she recalled the secretary saying the queen was waiting for her, with no mention of the king. She breathed a little easier. She hated disappointing her father, but it was different with her mother. She was used to disappointing her mother because it felt like nothing she ever did was good enough.

None of her past excursions had gone so wrong. She'd never once been escorted to an embassy, only to be sent home on a private plane surrounded by security. She wasn't sure if they were there to protect her or to make sure she didn't disappear again.

She stopped outside her mother's office door. She swallowed hard before drawing in a deep, calming breath. Before she could talk herself out of this, she rapped her knuckles on the door.

"Enter."

Cecelia opened the door and stepped inside. The room was dark except for the desk lamp that gave off a warm glow. Her mother was wearing a light blue satin robe. Her hair was still styled, but her makeup had been removed.

Her mother looked more her true age. The worry lines on her face were more evident. Cecelia wondered if she was partly responsible for her worries. Her and her siblings hadn't exactly been easy on their parents. They were each very strong-willed and independent.

Cecelia straightened her shoulders and prepared herself for a swift reprimand. "You wanted to see me."

Her mother removed her reading glasses

and studied Cecelia. A quick glance up and her eyes widened. "Your hair. What have you done to your beautiful hair? Please tell me it's a wig."

"It's not a wig."

Her mother frowned. The tense moment lingered. "Why would you do such a thing?"

Cecelia wasn't about to tell her mother that she'd done it in order to escape. "I needed a change."

Her mother was quiet for a moment. "But your long hair was so beautiful. Perhaps you could wear a wig until it grows in."

She shook her head. "I've had long hair my whole life. This short style is fun. I like it."

When the queen didn't immediately respond, Cecelia braced herself for her mother's negativity. It didn't matter what her mother said, she wasn't going to change her mind about wearing a wig. It was time she showed the kingdom that she was more than a dutiful, proper princess. The haircut was only the beginning of her transformation. She wanted to pursue her interest in fashion.

"The cut does highlight your face, but the color. Can we go back to your natural golden-brown shade?"

Was her mother negotiating with her? Cecelia stifled a smile. Usually her mother dictated the way things were going to be, but this time she had seen things Cecelia's way. And honestly, she was over the bleach blond color. "I'll change it back."

Her mother nodded her approval.

The king stepped forward. He gave Cecelia a start. She hadn't seen him sitting over in the shadows. He sent her a smile. "It's good that you're home." He approached her and gave her a quick hug. Then he turned back to her mother. "I'll let you two talk. Don't be too long."

"I won't," her mother said.

And then the king turned to Cecelia. "You have to stop worrying us. I'm getting too old for this sort of stuff."

"I'm sorry. I didn't mean to worry you."

He nodded. "Good night."

"'Night."

The door creaked open and then snicked shut behind him. Suddenly she wished that she had followed her father out the door.

Her mother's gaze probed her. "Where exactly have you been? We've been looking for you, especially after you didn't return when you told your sister you would."

And so Cecelia briefly told her mother about the accident and how for a few weeks she hadn't remembered anything. She didn't relay the part of her working as a housekeeper. She knew her mother would instantly dislike Antoine and she didn't want that to happen. For better or worse, he was the father of her baby. But that nugget of information could wait for another time.

"Are you alright?" The queen's eyes filled with concern.

"Yes, I'm fine now. My memory is still a bit fuzzy in places, but the doctor said it might not all come back at once."

Her mother reached for her desk phone. She called her private secretary. "Have the doctor come to the palace immediately." There was a slight pause. "No. It's for Princess Cecelia."

When her mother hung up, Cecelia said, "That isn't necessary. I've already seen a few doctors." She failed to mention that one of those doctors was an obstetrician. "And I had a bunch of tests done, which I passed."

"But those weren't our doctors. I just need to make sure you're alright."

Cecelia was surprised and touched by her mother's concern. "I'm sorry I worried you."

The queen sat behind her desk as a frown puckered her brow and pulled at her lips. "Of all the times for you to go off on one of your excursions, did it have to be when we're trying to deal with your brother walking away from the crown?"

Cecelia should have known that her mother's moment of caring wouldn't last long. Everything always came back to the crown and how the public perceived them. "That's part of the reason I needed to get away."

"What's that supposed to mean? I thought you left because you and... What was his name?"

"Paul."

"Yes. Because you'd stopped seeing each other."

"Mother, we didn't just break up. He dumped me because of the paparazzi." She wasn't sure her mother wanted to hear the truth, but Cecelia was going to give it to her, anyway. "You've been running the household ragged, trying to put on a show for the public so they believe all is the same in the palace now that Istvan isn't going to be king, but it's not the same. Nothing you do will make things the way they used to be."

The queen leaned back in her chair. "You just don't understand. There are certain expectations for this family."

"I understand those expectations. I've been dealing with them my whole life, but you know what I learned while I was in France?"

The queen's gaze narrowed in on her. "I have a feeling you're going to tell me."

"I've learned that without communication, families fall apart. So this is me trying to talk to you and hoping you'll truly hear me."

"Of course, I hear you. I always hear you."

"You only hear the parts you want to hear."

"This outburst is all because of that man in France—the one in the photos of you. He put these thoughts in your head, didn't he?"

"His name is Antoine and he didn't put any thoughts in my head. I came to these conclusions all on my own."

The queen sighed. "You're giving me a headache. Go to your bed chamber. The doctor should be here shortly to make sure you're alright."

Cecelia turned and headed for the door, happy to end this conversation. At the door, she glanced over her shoulder. "Good night."

Her mother didn't respond.

Cecelia opened the door and moved swiftly into the hallway. She pulled the door shut behind her. Maybe she should have told her mother about the baby, but she still needed time to figure out what her world would look like with a baby in it. And her mother was in no mood for such news.

She bounded up the grand staircase as fast

as she could. She strode to her room. She closed the door and leaned back against it. She couldn't keep her secret about the baby for long, but she just needed a few more days.

She wondered what Antoine was doing now. Was he thinking of her? Or was he relieved that she was gone from his life? The thought of never talking to Antoine again weighed heavy on her. Surely, he wouldn't write them both off, would he? The thought of Antoine repeating history by not being a part of his child's life made her heart ache.

Her arms wrapped around her midsection. "Don't worry, little one. I will always love you with all of my heart."

CHAPTER SIXTEEN

EARLY THE NEXT MORNING, the private jet touched down in Rydiania.

Antoine had been unusually tense the whole flight. Even though he'd brought his laptop with him, he hadn't gotten a bit of work done. He kept getting lost in his thoughts of Cecelia. He hadn't realized how much she'd come to mean to him until suddenly she was whisked away.

He had a car waiting for him. He didn't want to waste any time getting to Cecelia. She couldn't just disappear from his life without speaking directly to him. After all, she was having his baby.

Now he was stopped at the palace's front gate.

Antoine was not pleased that the Rydianian royal guards stopped him at the gate and would not let him onto the palace grounds. They wouldn't even call Cecelia. It was such an abrupt dismissal, as though they'd known he was coming and had been instructed to turn him away.

When he refused to leave, he was told to wait while the guard attended to other vehicles that passed by him and were permitted onto the palace grounds. His knee bounced up and down. This was absolutely ridiculous. If someone would just speak to Cecelia, she would vouch for him.

After two other vehicles were ushered through the gate without a thorough interrogation, and close to a half hour had passed, he was still stuck on the side of the roadway. He stared through the gate at the winding road surrounded by colorful gardens, but the palace was out of view.

When a different guard approached his vehicle, Antoine said, "My name is Antoine Dupré. I would like to see Cher— Erm… Princess Cecelia."

"Is she expecting you?"

"No. But if you just talk to her, I'm sure she'll want to see me." He wasn't so sure she would be anxious to see him, but that wasn't going to deter him.

Again, he was told to wait. The royal guardsman returned to his shack and this time made a phone call, presumably to the princess. At last, he was making progress.

The royal guardsman returned. "The princess will not see you."

That couldn't be possible. "Did you tell her it was me?"

"Yes, sir."

Would she really turn him away without hearing him out? "Let me talk to her."

"Please leave, sir."

"But I need to speak to her. It's urgent."

"Sir, you must leave now or you will be arrested." The guard's expression was serious.

They didn't mess around here. And as much as Antoine wanted to force his way through that gate to get to Cecelia, he knew getting arrested would not help his case. He had to bide his time and reach her another way.

And so, with the greatest of regret, he asked the driver to turn around and head into the nearby village. He noticed that as soon as they'd made the three-point turn, there was a black sedan behind them. He didn't doubt that it was security making sure he left without causing any further problems. What exactly had Cecelia told them about him?

In the village, he secured a room for the week at a small inn. He wasn't sure how long it was going to take for him to speak with the princess. *The princess*. It still shocked him that she was royalty.

As he was sitting at a small table not eating his dinner, he had a thought. He called his assistant, Margo. "I need your help."

"Sure. What do you need?"

"I need you to track down Princess Cecelia of Rydiania's schedule this week." He had no idea if her schedule was published. It was doubtful. But surely there would be mentions of events she was attending in the news.

"Okay. I'll see what I can find out."

"And then I need you to get me tickets to one of the events. I don't care what it costs or what favors I have to call in. This is urgent."

He wasn't leaving Rydiania without speaking to Cecelia. He had something important to tell her—something he hoped would make a difference.

She didn't want to be all dressed up.

She didn't want to be out in public.

And yet, Princess Cecelia wouldn't be anywhere else. Tonight was the Extraordinary Children's Art Awards dinner. It was an event that meant a lot to her. She just loved seeing the smiles on the children who hadn't given up on life because of the physical challenges that had been put in their way. They were an inspiration to her.

And now that her memory was fully intact, she was back to her royal duties. It was such a relief to recall her past. She even remembered her seventh birthday, when she'd begged her parents for a bouncy house. It had been placed on the south lawn. The bouncy house had been a big hit at her birthday party until she was in it with Beatrix when there was a big leak. The house collapsed quickly, trapping her and her sister. The king had dived inside to rescue them.

She remembered all of her subsequent birthdays. And most of all, she remembered all of her time with Antoine in agonizing detail that sometimes would bring tears to her eyes. She'd tried to convince herself that theirs was a brief fling. And yet she missed him so much—even if he didn't want her and the baby.

She shoved aside the troubling thoughts. Right now, she had to focus on her duties. She stood off to the side of the stage as she was introduced. She was to make a short speech before presenting awards to the children who had made extraordinary strides in the arts.

"Please welcome Her Royal Highness, Princess Cecelia."

And that was her cue to step onto the stage. She took careful steps up the stairs so as not to trip. Now that she was pregnant, she was aware of all the ways she could get hurt. The whole world looked different to her now.

Loud applause filled the hall as she approached the microphone. For a moment, the spotlights combined with camera flashes blinded her. She blinked and refocused.

"I am honored to be here with some of the world's finest and youngest artists. They are courageous. They are determined. They are extraordinary."

As she continued with her speech, her gaze adjusted to the dimmed lighting. She glanced around at the smiling children all dressed up in their finest, accompanied by their families. She loved being a part of this fabulous foundation.

She didn't know what the future held for her child, but she took comfort in knowing that organizations such as this existed to celebrate the lives of these children. They gave her such hope for the future of this world.

"And now I would like to share with you images of these award-winning works of art, as well as present the artists with their award—" Her words faltered as her gaze connected with a very familiar set of intense brown eyes.

Her heart leaped into her throat. *Antoine.* She blinked, but he was still sitting at a table near the stage. What was he doing here? The very expensive tickets for patrons had sold out long ago. For him to be here, he had to be very well connected.

The lights darkened as the first image appeared on the large screen behind her. In the darkness, she was no longer able to stare into his eyes. Someone cleared their throat. It spurred her back into action.

She introduced the title of the drawing of an elderly man feeding six homeless kittens. The details were exquisite and it was filled with emotion. It showed how everyone had a role to play in life. And most astounding, it was drawn by a ten-year-old.

When the lights came back up again, her gaze moved to the table where she'd seen Antoine. Now there was nothing but an empty seat. Where had he gone? Her gaze scanned the area, as she did her best to act and speak as though nothing was wrong, even though her world felt as though it had just spun off its axis.

Throughout the rest of the ceremony, she scanned the audience for any sign of Antoine. She didn't see him again. And by the end of the program, she'd convinced herself that it had all been a figment of her imagination. She must have mistaken someone else for him.

She breathed easier as she descended the stairs. She was greeted by the head of the organization. She was thanked for her generosity, not only for her time, but also the donation she'd made from her personal funds.

When she finally shook the last hand and smiled her last smile, she was ready to go home. She turned toward the back exit only to find Antoine standing between her and the hallway to the rear exit.

Her mouth opened but no words came out. Her heart beat faster. There was a part of her that wanted to rush to him and wrap her arms around him, but the other part of her stood her ground. She wasn't going to throw herself at a man who had, for all intents and purposes, rejected her.

She straightened her shoulders and lifted her chin until their gazes met. And she waited for him to speak.

"Hello, Cherie. Excuse me… Princess Cecelia." He bowed his head.

"How did you get in here? It's a private function."

"I bought a ticket."

She didn't believe him. Whom did he know besides her in Rydiania? "From whom?"

His eyes glittered with amusement at her frustration. "A friend of a friend. But I don't think that's what you want to know."

She crossed her arms. "What are you doing here?"

"I came to see you."

"Why? We said everything that needed to be said."

"No, we haven't. Not even close."

What was he getting at? Was he worried she would acknowledge his paternity to the world? The thought of him wanting to deny his own child deeply saddened her.

She was radiant.

And was she taller? Not possible. But the way she now carried herself gave that impression.

Antoine couldn't take his gaze off Cecelia all evening. Even though it'd been less than a week, he'd missed her terribly. He drank in her vision.

One thing that had changed about her was the color of her hair. It was now a golden brown. There was something else different about her. He just couldn't put his finger on it.

And then it came to him. It was her confidence. She knew exactly who she was—a princess of Rydiania. All of her unending questions had been answered. She was certain of who she was and where she fit into the world. He was so happy for her. But he also worried about the divide that her being royal would put between them.

A spark of anger glinted in her eyes. She may have remembered her past, but she hadn't forgotten their last words. He had a lot of work ahead of him.

"Can we go somewhere to talk in private?" He glanced around at all of the people lingering nearby.

"No." Her eyebrows drew together as she frowned at him. "You need to leave. Now."

He shook his head as he stood his ground. "You aren't going to turn me away like you did at the palace."

"At the palace? I don't know what you're talking about."

Interesting. "The morning after you left Paris. I flew to Rydiania, only to be turned away at the gate."

Confusion reflected in her eyes. "I don't know what you're talking about. You came to see me? But why?"

"Because I didn't like the way we left

things. How are you? Has your memory returned?"

"I'm fine. My memory is back and I remember you telling me that you aren't interested in having a family of your own."

Her pointed words poked at a tender spot in his chest. Even though he wanted both her and the baby back, he still had his reservations about fatherhood. "When I said those words, it was before I knew you were pregnant."

Before he could say more, she was approached by a burly man in a dark suit. He had an earpiece, which indicated he was a bodyguard. The man kept his back to the princess as he continually surveilled the group of people. "Your Highness, it's time for us to go."

"I just need a moment." When the man moved a discreet distance away, she asked again, "Why are you here?"

"Because I want you back. I want the baby."

She shook her head. "Don't."

"Cecelia, I'm serious."

Her narrowed gaze settled on him. "What has changed?"

What did she mean? Everything had changed. "You left."

"Not what has changed with me, but what

has changed with you? Why do you suddenly want to be a father?"

He paused. The truth was he didn't have a good answer. He still didn't know what it was to be a good father. But he could learn. Couldn't he?

"I don't think you know what you want." Her unflinching gaze bore into his. "I have to go."

"But what about us?"

"There is no us. There is the baby, and we can discuss him or her later. Not now." And with that, she began walking for the exit.

As quickly as the discussion had begun, it had ended. He should go after her, but he didn't move. He had been dismissed by the princess. She didn't want him and that stung. It more than stung. Her sharp words sliced through him. They struck much deeper than he'd ever felt something before.

He had lost his opportunity to be a husband and father. It was something he hadn't realized until that moment that he wanted with all his heart and soul. And his chance had just walked out the door.

There was nothing more he could do right now. Maybe what he needed to do was unravel the secrets of his past—maybe then he would be able to find a new path forward.

He needed to get away. The more he thought about it, the more determined he was to go to Australia. He would track down his own father. He had questions, so many questions, starting with why his father had decided he didn't want him after all.

If he could understand his father, maybe he could avoid making the same mistakes with his own child. Because Cecelia may not want him in her life, but he promised himself that he would be a regular presence in his own child's life.

CHAPTER SEVENTEEN

TWO WEEKS...

Technically, fifteen days...

That was how long it'd been since Cecelia had last seen Antoine. It felt more like forever. A part of her regretted turning him away. Maybe she shouldn't have been so hasty. After all, there was so much she wanted to share with him about the baby.

Sometimes she let herself forget how things had ended between them. When she got excited about something new she learned about the baby, she'd automatically reach for her phone. With his phone number not saved on her phone, she'd be immediately brought back to reality. At other times, the feeling of loneliness could be so overwhelming.

Apparently, her unhappiness was obvious to the rest of her family. When Beatrix was set to travel to Rome for a couple of weeks to attend some social engagements, Cecelia was encouraged to go. At first, she'd resisted. She hadn't wanted to be seen in public and wear a fake smile. In the end, she'd accompanied her sister, but she'd never left their Italian villa. Instead, she'd spent her time by the pool, reliving the memories of the time she'd spent in France with Antoine.

Now the trip was over and they were headed back to Rydiania. Between thoughts of the baby and how much she missed Antoine, Cecelia was quiet on the plane ride. Beatrix had tried making conversation but eventually decided to leave Cecelia to her thoughts. Cecelia thought of confiding in her sister about the baby. She knew she couldn't put off the news of her pregnancy forever. She had to tell her family sooner rather than later. But she wasn't ready—not yet.

Their chauffeured car pulled up at the palace and the sisters got out. When Cecelia noticed the queen waiting for them, she had an uneasy feeling. Their mother wasn't one to anxiously stand around waiting for her grown children to return home. She had more important matters to attend to. So for the queen to be waiting meant that something had happened.

Side by side, the sisters approached their

mother, who didn't smile. An uneasy feeling churned in the pit of Cecelia's stomach.

Her mother's gaze met hers. "Cecelia, we need to talk."

Immediately her mind circled around to her pregnancy. Did she know? No. Impossible. Cecelia had taken great pains not to have any blood work done when her mother had insisted on a thorough exam that included another brain scan, which came back clear.

"Is there something wrong?" Cecelia asked.

"We need to have this conversation in my office."

That alone didn't worry Cecelia. Her mother was all about privacy, even if it pertained to some detail for her brother's wedding. Yes, that must be it because the wedding was only mere months away.

She followed her mother to her office and closed the door behind them. Her mother didn't sit at her desk, as was her custom. Instead, the queen sat on the couch.

Cecelia sat on one of the chairs. "What do you need?"

"I had some tea made for us. Would you like a cup?"

She swallowed hard. She recalled her mother's saying that difficult conversations were best held with a cup a tea, as there were things to stir and sip. "Yes, please."

Once the tea had been poured, and a bit of sugar and cream added, her mother held on to her cup as she sat back on the couch. "How are you feeling?"

"Fine." Her morning sickness had settled now that it was early afternoon. However, at this particular moment she wasn't feeling particularly well. Her stomach fluttered with nerves as she waited for her mother to get to the point of this conversation.

The queen studied her. "You haven't looked quite like yourself since you've returned. I thought some time in Rome would have put the color back in your cheeks and yet you still look pale. Maybe I should ring the doctor again."

"No. That isn't necessary. I wasn't in the sun much." She'd sat beneath a big umbrella next to the pool.

"Your sister said you didn't attend any of the events."

"I didn't realize I was expected to attend any of them."

"You weren't. I just thought you might grow bored of the villa and want to get out for a while."

"I was fine. I had some books to read."

Her mother looked at her outfit. "It doesn't look like you've been sewing, either."

"Excuse me?"

"Your clothes, they don't look like you've modified them. I know it sometimes drives me a little nutty, but you do have a knack for fashion."

"I do? I mean, you think so? You've never said anything before."

"It seems I assumed my children knew my thoughts. I'll have to rely more on my words." She sipped at her tea. "So why haven't you been sewing?"

Cecelia shrugged. "I haven't felt like it."

"Perhaps I could have some new material ordered and placed in your room. Maybe some brightly colored patterns. I know how you love color. Would you like that?"

"Thanks. But no." Her inspiration had fled her and she didn't know when it'd return.

"Cecelia, I know you have something weighing on your mind. Would you like to talk about it?"

This was her opening. It was almost as though her mother already knew about her pregnancy, but that wasn't possible. Her clothes were a little tight but not to the point where she was showing.

Cecelia knew it was best to say it now and

get it over with, but the words clogged in the back of her throat. She knew this pregnancy would create another scandal for the palace…at the very worst time. With her brother's wedding not far off, she didn't want to do anything to tarnish it.

And yet trying to keep this pregnancy hidden was only going to work for so long. Eventually she would begin to show.

And so she swallowed hard, straightened her shoulders and lifted her chin ever so slightly. Her gaze met her mother's. "I'm pregnant."

The queen didn't move. Her facial expression didn't change. Cecelia wasn't even sure that she breathed. It was though her mother hadn't heard what she'd said. She thought she'd uttered the words clearly. Perhaps she hadn't.

"Mother, I'm pregnant."

The queen blinked. "I heard you. May I presume it occurred while you were in France?"

"Yes."

Her mother was being so calm that it made Cecelia more nervous than if her mother had exploded and unleashed the full weight of her disappointment on her.

"The father, his name is Antoine?"

"How did you know?"

"Because it was in the news and he came here to see you the day after you returned."

So what Antoine had said was true. "Why is this the first I'm hearing of it?"

"Because I didn't want your recovery hampered. You hadn't mentioned him so I figured he wasn't important to you, otherwise you would have alerted the staff to admit him."

Cecelia lifted her cup to take a sip of her tea, but her stomach heaved at the thought. She immediately lowered it.

"This Antoine Dupré, he cares for you deeply?"

Cecelia shook her head. "He only sought me out because he feels a duty to the baby."

"So he knows about the child?"

She nodded. "We found out just before we traveled to Paris. But he told me he doesn't want children."

"Maybe he changed his mind."

She shook her head again. "I don't think so."

"Learning you're going to be a parent sometimes comes as a shock. I remember when I told your father I was pregnant with your brother. It was days before our wedding and your father hadn't been expecting to become a father so soon. It took him a bit to come to terms with the idea and then he was delighted. Perhaps that's what happened with Antione."

Cecelia gaped at her mother. Had she heard her correctly? Surely not. Her mother was the master of decorum, order and etiquette.

"Don't look so shocked," her mother said. "Do you really think you young people are the first to discover passion? Your father was always a passionate lover—"

"Mother!" Heat flamed in Cecelia's cheeks.

What was wrong with her mother? She never talked this way. Cecelia felt as though she was in some sort of warped dream and she was unable to wake up.

The queen smiled. "And here I was thinking you were all grown up."

"I am. But that doesn't mean I want to hear anything about you and Father. Not about that stuff." Her face felt scorched from the heat of embarrassment.

"Alright. I understand. But have you considered giving Antoine another chance? I know that he cares greatly for you."

"How do you know?"

"Once he showed up at the palace, I had him checked out. And then when he showed up again at the awards dinner, my sources said he couldn't take his eyes off you all evening. He cares for you a lot." Her mother's laser vision focused pointedly on her. "And you care for him. It's written all over your face."

Cecelia thought of denying it, but what was the point? "Yes, I do care about him."

"It's more than that. You love him, don't you?"

The answer was so much easier for her than she ever imagined. "Yes, I do. But I don't know if he feels the same way. I was so afraid of being hurt again that I sent him away without hearing him out."

Her mother didn't react at first. She lifted her cup, but before she took a drink, she said, "I assumed that was the case and that's why the jet is ready. Your security team is standing by. It's time you go talk to Antoine."

She couldn't believe her ears. "You aren't going to fight me?"

Her mother returned the teacup to the saucer without having taken a drink. "I like to think that I am smart enough to learn from my mistakes. I fought with your brother when he fell in love with Indigo. It only forced him further away. We're still working on patching up things. I don't want that with you."

Sometimes her mother really did surprise her. Cecelia set aside her tea and stood. Her mother did the same. She couldn't help but smile. "Thank you for being so understanding."

"I don't have much of a choice. One scandal is enough for this family. Now go. I have work to do."

Cecelia knew her mother normally showed a stiff and proper demeanor, but sometimes her heart really shone through. This was one of those times.

She moved to her mother. She kissed her cheek and hugged her. Her mother hugged her back.

When Cecelia pulled back, she said, "I love you."

"I love you, too. Now go be happy."

Cecelia didn't have to be told twice. She was out the door. With her luggage still in the foyer, she grabbed it and hurried outside. She had a flight to catch and a man to win back.

CHAPTER EIGHTEEN

HE MISSED HER.

He missed her terribly.

And that's why he'd flown to Australia with his investigator to find his father and demand an explanation for why he had been absent from his life. Antoine couldn't imagine that his father would have a good enough explanation to excuse his absence, but he'd been willing to hear him out.

They'd started with the address from the letter. His investigator was able to recover the original address beneath the smudge. The current resident didn't have a clue who had written the letter. They gave them the name of the prior owners. It took a bit to track them down.

The family claimed they didn't own the house the year Antoine was born, but they did some searching and found a document with the previous family's name. Then it was time for his investigator to do his thing.

It had been an amazing couple of weeks, but now Antoine was back in France. He wondered how Cecelia was doing—if she ever thought of him. Numerous times he'd thought of calling her—of telling her how much he cared about her—but he didn't allow himself that luxury. She'd already rejected him. The memory still hurt deeply.

It was better they didn't speak. He needed the time to adjust to his life without her in it. And that started with him selling the château. His life was in Paris, not meandering around in this big, old house all by himself.

When he walked into the kitchen, he imagined seeing Cecelia in one of those sexy little housekeeper uniforms. When he looked at the guesthouse, he wanted to go there to visit with her. And when he came in from the fields at the end of a long day, he hoped to run into her.

Instead, the kitchen was empty and there was no reason to make a quick run into the village for the fresh croissants she loved so much. The guesthouse would remain empty and there would be no more sunset dinners on the balcony. She wasn't there to make him smile after a hard day of work in the fields. There was absolutely no reason to keep this house full of memories.

It was time to accept reality.

Antoine stood in the kitchen of the château. The entire house was now clean from top to bottom. He didn't think they'd done as good of a job as Cecelia. She'd wanted to make a good impression on him and she had worked so hard that she'd made things shine.

It wasn't until she was gone that he realized the depth of his emotions. He loved Cecelia. He loved how her smile warmed him from the inside out. He loved how determined she could be when something was important to her. And he loved how she'd showed him that there was so much more to life than his work.

Why hadn't he realized all of this sooner? He inwardly groaned. Maybe then she wouldn't have left and he wouldn't be missing her now.

The truth was that he'd never had these emotions for anyone else. When he'd seen her in Rydiania at the charity function, just the sight of her had made his heart beat faster. He'd fooled himself into thinking if he went after her that she would fall into his arms and they'd live happily ever after. He hadn't paused long enough to think that she might not feel the same way, especially after remembering she was a princess.

He was going to have to get over that because she wasn't coming back. Why would she? He couldn't offer her a life of royalty and glamour. He may be wealthy, but he didn't have the connections her family had.

"Is there a problem with the contract?" The man's voice drew Antoine from his thoughts.

He glanced down at the stack of papers in front of him. He'd been over them. His attorney had been over them. Everything was in order. To list the property for sale, all he had to do was sign.

And yet he hesitated. He now understood the grief that had existed between these walls as he'd been growing up. It was all so much clearer to him now than when he'd been living through it all.

His grandparents had never gotten over the loss of their daughter. His grandmother had spoiled him with all of her pent-up love. His grandfather had loved him but didn't show it. Instead, he tried to protect Antoine by pulling on the reins too tightly. His mother died for the love of him and his father.

This house was filled with a history of love. He'd been too young to realize it at the time. Love wasn't always displayed in the same manner—sometimes it went astray.

He hoped the next family that lived here

would fill the house once again with love. And then he picked up the pen and signed the papers.

He placed them in the envelope and handed them back to the real-estate agent. "Will it take long?"

The man shook his head. "Not at all. A place like this is a gem. It will go quickly."

"Good. I don't want this to drag out."

"It won't. I'll be in contact."

They were on their way to the door when there was a knock. He wasn't expecting anyone. And the For Sale sign hadn't been hung.

Antoine moved to the door and swung open the door. He couldn't believe what he was seeing. Cecelia. She'd come back.

Her heart was racing.

Cecelia was standing outside the château. Her palms grew damp. Even if Antoine had wanted her back when he was in Rydiania, which had been a couple of weeks ago, would he have changed his mind by now?

Even so, she had stipulations before she'd let herself get involved with him again. He had to truly love her. It was something they'd never discussed before. But she knew she didn't want him taking her back out of duty.

She knew all about how things went wrong when people acted out of duty instead of out of love. Her family was littered with personal disasters because people acted in accordance with their duty to the crown. She'd never once seen where duty had led to happiness.

And this decision about their future was too important to their child's happiness to get it wrong. The only chance they had for a lasting relationship was if it was based on love. Without love, they'd falter and fail.

She'd never been more anxious in her entire life. She glanced over her shoulder at her security team. She'd insisted they remain outside. This was a conversation that needed to be done in private.

Her heart pounded as her anxiety rose. What would she do if he told her he didn't love her? She couldn't go back to the palace pregnant and alone. She refused to become yet another royal scandal. She would not let that happen to her baby.

She would have to move away to somewhere quiet—a place where she could give her child a warm and loving life. But she was jumping too far ahead. She needed to talk to Antoine first.

"Hello, Antoine." She sent him a tentative smile as she drank in his handsomeness.

He nodded in acknowledgment but didn't say a word.

She hadn't anticipated a warm welcome after the way she'd turned him away at the awards dinner, but she hadn't expected him not to speak to her at all. For a moment, an awkward silence ensued.

"Well, I should be going." A shorter man stepped out from the shadows. He held his hand out to Antoine. They shook. "It's been good doing business with you. I'll be in touch."

Then the man turned to her, smiled and nodded. She moved aside to let him out the door. And then she turned back to Antoine. His expression was blank. He wasn't going to make this easy for her.

"May I come in?" she asked.

He gestured toward the driveway. "What about them?"

She glanced over her shoulder at her security team. "They are fine out there." When he still didn't move aside, she said, "Could we please talk...in private?"

He hesitated a moment longer before he stepped back, allowing her to pass by him. She entered, moving slowly, and took in the familiar scent of his spicy cologne mingled with his manly scent. She inhaled deeply. Boy, had she missed him.

It was tempting to stop and take a closer whiff, but now wasn't the time for that. She briefly paused in the foyer, trying to decide where it would be best to have this conversation.

She opted for the kitchen. They'd spent a lot of time there and most of it had been good—some of it had been very good indeed. Maybe the happy memories in there would help them with this difficult conversation.

She moved to the kitchen table. And then she remembered what her mother had said about having a warm drink for difficult conversations.

"Can I make you some coffee?" she asked. And then she realized she didn't have the right to be so forward in his kitchen.

"I just made some. I'll get us a cup." He paused and turned to her. "Are you allowed to have coffee while you're pregnant?"

"The doctor said one cup a day." She'd done a lot of reading about her pregnancy. She wanted to do everything right, including patching things up with the father of her baby. "I'll get the cream and sugar."

"I can get those. You can sit down."

She opened her mouth to say she didn't

need him to wait on her, but she realized that arguing with him wouldn't help matters, so she pulled out a chair and had a seat.

Antoine placed a cup of coffee in front of her with sugar and cream. She set about fixing her coffee just the way she liked it. All the while she was trying to decide where to start this conversation.

When he finally sat down across from her, she swallowed hard. "I'm sorry I wouldn't hear you out when you came to Rydiania. It was wrong of me."

His gaze searched hers. "Why are you here now?"

"Because we owe it to our child to see if there is something real between the two of us."

"And it took you until now to figure this out?"

She shook her head. "I've tried to call you, but it always went to voice mail."

"I've been out of the country."

She nodded. "When I couldn't reach you, I called your assistant. She told me you were on an extended trip. Did you go to find your father?"

"I did. My investigator was able track down the name of my family. They don't live far from the original house that was listed on the return address. I'm not normally a nervous person, but I was a bit anxious about facing my long-lost family."

"That must have been so surreal for you. I'm sorry I wasn't there with you."

"At the beginning, I let my investigator do a lot of the talking."

"Were they excited to meet you?" When he smiled and nodded, she asked, "Was your father there?"

"No. I never got to meet him. He died in a plane crash while on his way to France the day I was born."

Cecelia gasped. "Oh, Antoine. I'm so very sorry. But at least now you know that he really did love you and your mother."

"Yes. So many of my questions were answered. And now my family consists of aunts, uncles and lots of cousins. They eagerly welcomed me, a perfect stranger, into their family. They showed me such kindness and love. And so my investigator returned to Paris and I remained in Australia for a couple of weeks. They showed me old photos—so many photos. I actually resemble my father." He pulled up a photo on his phone to show her.

"You really do look a lot like him."

"And they told me stories about him. He was always active. He loved to play sports, and when he went to the university, he studied business."

"It's amazing how alike you two are. I wonder if our child will also have a head for business."

"I'm okay if he...or she wants to do something different. As long as it's honest work that fulfills them, I'll be happy."

Cecelia reached out and squeezed his hand. "I agree."

"When it came time for me to leave Australia, it was hard for me to do. There were lots of hugs, some tears and lots of promises to see each other again soon. I offered to fly them to Paris at the holidays. And in turn, I promised to return in the New Year. I'd like it if you'd consider coming with me."

A big smile pulled at her lips. "You would?"

He nodded. "And I would love nothing better than to have you with me."

She smiled through her happy tears. "You would?"

"Definitely. But we still have a problem."

"What's that?"

"I just put the château up for sale."

"No. You can't sell it."

"You do know my real-estate agent is going to be very disappointed?"

"He'll get over it. There's not a chance I'm

giving up the view from the balcony." Her happiness screeched to a halt as she realized they still had a huge problem. Without love, none of this was going to work.

His eyebrows drew together. "What's wrong?"

"This isn't going to work."

"Sure it is. I love you."

Her eyes widened as her heart momentarily lodged in her throat. She'd been waiting so long for him to say those words. But could she believe him? Was he just saying what he thought she wanted to hear?

She swallowed hard. "You do?"

A smile tugged at the corners of his lips. "I definitely do. With all of my heart."

Inwardly she was swooning, but she refused to fall into his arms just yet. "And you aren't just saying this because I'm pregnant?"

He shook his head. "I'm saying this because I was a fool and let you get away the first time. I'd never felt so alone as when you walked away from me at that charity event." He reached out and caressed her cheek. "I'm so sorry I hurt you. I will spend the rest of my days making it up to you and showing you just how much I love you."

He was saying all of the right words, but she had to be certain. After all, it wasn't just her future on the line, but also their baby's. "What about your business in Paris? I don't want a part-time marriage."

He stared into her eyes. "Neither do I. That's why I've been considering the idea of selling the business and devoting my time to my family and the vineyard."

She gasped. "Are you serious? I mean I don't want you giving up the business you built from the ground up because you think it's what I want. I don't want you to resent me some day."

"I could never resent you. I love you way too much. But my business doesn't bring me the satisfaction that it once did. I've found that I like working outside. I love the smell of the earth and the feel of the sun on my back. The only reason I was going to sell this place was because you weren't here to share it with me."

"Aww…well, I'm here now and forever, if you'll have me."

He pulled her close. "I'm never letting you go again. I love you."

"I love you, too." She lifted up on her tip-toes and pressed her lips to his.

He might not know how to be a good father, but with Cecelia's help, he hoped to learn to be one. Along the way, he may have had his worries about parenthood, but his mother and father had helped him realize that he was capable of more than he ever imagined.

EPILOGUE

Seven months later...

HIS ROYAL HIGHNESS PRINCE MARKOS slept in his father's arms. Cecelia watched as the two most important men in her life bonded. Markos looked like a little angel. No one would ever suspect that he'd just cried his head off for the last twenty minutes because...well, she wasn't quite sure what had caused his unhappiness. He'd just been fed, burped and changed.

But now the little tyke was sound asleep and looking utterly angelic. Markos was born with a full head of dark hair and the most striking blue eyes. He was a charmer from the very start.

"He's so quiet," Beatrix said.

"Just wait until two o'clock tonight," Antoine said. "When he gets hungry, he gets mad until he gets some food in his tummy."

Cecelia was so happy her sister had come to visit and help them with the baby. Although her sister knew even less about caring for a newborn than she did. It would be a learning experience for the both of them.

"Mother and Father are so anxious for you two to bring this little fellow to the palace." Beatrix leaned closer to take a better look. "And Gisella won't say it, but I know she's jealous that I was the first to see him. She thought being the crown princess was going to be so great, but even she's finding that it has its drawbacks."

Cecelia didn't say it but their older sister was born to be a leader. She had always been bossing them around. It would be interesting to see her step into the role of queen. Although Cecelia and her family would be doing it from a distance as the château had become their full-time home.

Antoine stood with the baby. "I'm just going to put him in the nursery."

Beatrix got to her feet. "Can I take him?"

"Sure." Antoine ever so gently transferred their sleeping son into her sister's arms.

Beatrix's face lit up with happiness. She looked so good with a baby in her arms. Something told Cecelia that it wouldn't be long until her sister had a baby of her own.

Cecelia stood and went to her husband. She wrapped her arms around his waist and lifted up on her tiptoes to give him a kiss. When she pulled back, she said, "We made a really cute baby, didn't we?"

"We certainly did. How about having another one?"

She gasped. "We just had Markos. He's not even a week old and you're already talking about another baby."

"Okay. I see your point. We can wait until next month to start trying."

"Antoine, you're incorrigible."

A big smile came over his face and lit up his eyes. "But you love me."

"Yes, I do. But another baby is going to have to wait a bit."

"Okay. I don't mind practicing." He leaned over and kissed the sensitive part of her neck.

"Neither do I. I love you."

He lifted his head and stared deeply into her eyes. "Always and forever."

* * * * *

*Look out for the next story in the
Princesses of Rydiania trilogy,*
Royal Mom for the Duke's Daughter,
coming soon!

*And if you enjoyed this story,
check out these other great reads
from Jennifer Faye*

Greek Heir to Claim Her Heart
It Started with a Royal Kiss
Second Chance with the Bridesmaid

All available now!